Mara Menzies is a narrative artist who draws on her rich, dual Kenyan/Scottish cultural heritage to create worlds that explore contemporary issues through legend, myth and fantasy. Her storytelling performance *Blood and Gold*, which inspired this book, premiered at the Edinburgh Festival Fringe in 2019 to rapturous praise. She has toured in 27 countries.

Eri Griffin is a freelance illustrator based in Edinburgh who works with publishers and design agencies across the UK and Europe.

Blood and Gold

A Journey of Shadows

MARA MENZIES

Illustrated by ERI GRIFFIN

BIRLINN

First published in 2021 by
Birlinn Limited
West Newington House
10 Newington Road
Edinburgh
EH9 1QS

www.birlinn.co.uk

ISBN: 978 1 78027 746 2

British Library Cataloguing-in-Publication Data
A catalogue record for this book is available
from the British Library

Designed and typeset by Mark Blackadder

Printed and bound by Bell & Bain Ltd, Glasgow

For my nyanya, who is watching from another world.
For my mother, who is here now.
For Imani and Barasa, who are the future.
With love

A young black man once travelled to Edinburgh for a meeting and sat down at a cafe on the Royal Mile. The waiter pulled out his seat and called him 'sir'. He was struck by how equal he felt, as he had never encountered such hospitality before.

Another young black man found himself in the Grassmarket, a beautiful, enjoyable part of the city. He had the audacity to speak to a white woman, an act for which he was stabbed to death and, despite the many eyewitnesses and the known identities of the killers, nobody was ever brought to justice.

The first story took place in 1846 – 175 years ago. The young man was Sir Frederick Douglass. He had escaped slavery in the Americas and became one of the foremost anti-slavery campaigners of his time. The second story took place in 1989, not too long ago. The young man was Axmed Sheekh, a promising young student from Somalia.

It's surprising how little we have moved forward. It is not surprising how little we talk about it because it is uncomfortable to believe that Scots were the majority shareholders in the plantations. It is unsettling to think that many Scottish families benefited from millions of pounds in compensation from the British government for the 'loss' of their human property. It is an unpalatable truth that 70 per cent of the Jamaican telephone directory is made up of Scottish names. It is easier to shy away from the fact that portraying black people as sub-human was essential for the success of the colonies and the slave trade, and how in many ways that narrative is perpetuated to this day.

Who would want to speak about things like that? But the thing is, we need to. Because if we don't talk about it, acknowledge it and learn from it, then the increasing hate crimes, intolerance and racism that we see everywhere will seep further into our society, and a society filled with fear and hate is a lost society. I love our country and I imagine a better future for us.

Mara

HOW THE STORY BEGINS

It took Rahami, Jeda's mother, two hundred and eighty-three days to die. Two hundred and eighty-three days from the moment Dr Harrison first told her she was sick to the moment Jeda placed her head on her mother's chest and gently felt her soul fly away. Jeda was eight years old. Her mother had held her close, stroking her hair and singing her favourite tune. The tune had grown fainter and fainter until Jeda could no longer hear it at all. She then noticed her head no longer rose and fell with her mother's breathing but lay as if resting on a warm pillow that had gradually lost its softness. It had been slow, as though Jeda's mother had simply given herself away.

At first Jeda didn't understand. Then her confusion slowly turned into a silent rage as she realised that her mother had lied. She had told her she would always be there, but she wasn't. She was gone.

Jeda looked around and saw the solemn faces of her father and Aunty. The little white room overlooked a cold, grey sea, and the tubes and plastic chairs suddenly felt like they were all closing in on her. She needed to get out. Now! She clenched her fists and felt every ugly thought, every bad word that she had ever heard, building up inside her, ready to explode. She wiped a strand of mucus from her nose, stood up and headed towards the door.

'Come, darling.' Aunty's words were as soft as the snowflakes falling outside. She reached out her arms to comfort the little girl, but Jeda pushed past her and raced into the corridor of the hospital where nobody ever seemed to get well. She was filled with rage at the sight of two nurses in blue uniforms sitting at their perfectly sanitised station having a chat. Their job was to keep people safe. They hadn't. Instead they were talking about their children, or last night's dinner, or some other entirely irrelevant event.

The bad words rose from her chest, through her throat, filling her mouth, wrapping themselves around her teeth, her tongue, her lips until finally they were released . . . a wave of filth that bounced off the pale blue walls. Jeda screamed them all. Every word she had heard on the television but wasn't allowed to repeat. The word that a boy in her class had used, landing him in trouble with their teacher. The word that her father had used when he was watching football one day and the other team scored. She understood that such words were used to express pain and anger or some other intense emotion, so now they poured out of her and it felt good. She screamed until there was nothing left, then stood there breathless. The nurses stared at her, open-mouthed in disbelief.

Aunty appeared in the corridor and called her name. Jeda bolted. She ran down the stairs towards the main door and pushed desperately against the glass, but it wouldn't open. A nurse arrived and asked if she needed help. Jeda whipped round and glared at her, baring her teeth like a trapped animal before diving through her legs in an attempt to escape. She kept running, running, till she found

herself in a place she suspected she wasn't supposed to be. It was not perfect like the rest of the building. The walls around her were of thick, grey stone and in the patches where there was plaster it peeled off in untidy strips.

She found herself at the bottom of an old, winding staircase with an intricately carved wooden handrail. Her footsteps echoed loudly as she sprinted up the steps, which eventually led to a long corridor. Frantically, she tried door after door, each one locked tight, until finally it seemed one took pity on her and creaked open. It led to a tiny broom cupboard, dark with thick cobwebs in the corners. She squeezed herself in, slamming the door behind her. She reached out gingerly, her fingers pushing everything they encountered to the side, creating a little space in the corner, where she wrapped her arms around her knees and sat. The only sound was that of her breathing as she tried not to gag at the odour of the musty old mops that surrounded her. As she tried not to think of anything at all.

•   •   •

It was a cold day for a burial, so it took place quickly. Rahami had insisted that she would return to the earth in her purest form. There was to be no embalming and she thought a simple cardboard coffin would do nicely. One on which those who wished to do so could inscribe messages of love and affection. She wanted a tree planted as tribute. Just a simple goodbye. Jeda's father had carried out Rahami's wishes with help from their friends. Jeda now thought how different this was to the burials that she had seen on television, where most people wore black – Rahami had insisted that this would be a celebration of life, so those who attended wore pinks and golds, blues and yellows. Chris had gently asked Jeda if she wanted to be there for the burial. Of course she did! How could her father ask such a thing?

However, as the celebrant raised one hand to the sky, she began to wonder if she had made the right choice, for a black crow settled on a branch above her. Although its head appeared to point away into the distance, Jeda couldn't shake the unpleasant sensation that it was staring right at her. She saw black clouds rolling across the sky. They cast terrible shadows on the coffin, which rested on the bright green grass.

'Real grass would have been better,' thought Jeda, annoyed at the artificial blades that were so horribly vibrant, in such stark contrast to the deep, black hole beside them.

When the pallbearers raised the coffin and began to lower it into the ground, the crow opened its beak and cawed loudly. Jeda felt something was terribly wrong. The hole was too dark. Her mother would not be able to see. The box was too small. How would she get out? This was wrong. All wrong. The crow must be an omen. The clouds, everything. She ran forward and tried to grab at the coffin.

'Mummy, Mummy!' she sobbed.

Her father was right behind her. He gently placed a hand on her shoulder, then knelt down.

'It's okay, darling. Mummy's resting! It's time for her to go.'

Jeda realised there was nothing more she could do, so she stood and simmered with anger and confusion as those around her threw handfuls of soil into the dark hole where her mother now lay. She wanted to yell at them all, but the hand on her shoulder reminded her that she was a good girl and certainly no troublemaker, so she forced the rage to remain within, slowly tightening around her gut.

In the weeks and months that followed, Jeda saw her father struggle. She found him clutching a framed photograph of Rahami, weeping in the living room. She didn't want him to be bothered any more than he needed, so she tried her hardest to be strong. She helped more around the house. She cooked the meals and tried to keep her room tidy. Her show of strength was so convincing it was easy for her father to believe that she was coping well.

But from behind the crevices in the walls, in the moments of restless sleep when she tried to pull her mother from the black hole that had swallowed her, the Shadowman was watching.

He could see the cracks in her soul.

He understood her rage.

And that was when he spotted an opportunity to slip into her world.

•   •   •

Jeda knew about the Shadowman long before she met him.

'Be aware, my darling,' her mother would say. 'He comes in many forms and can be hard to recognise. His greatest wish is to control you, so always be aware!'

At first he came to her as she slept, whispering to her and guiding her dreams. He conjured a beautiful picture of a princess with long, straight, icy-white hair and a golden crown.

'She's beautiful, isn't she?' he would ask, his voice soft and gentle.

'Yes,' Jeda would whisper, her eyes shut.

'The most beautiful in the world?' he suggested.

'Yes,' she would reply, believing it.

As the years went by, he began to watch her during the day, accompanying her wherever she went. He fed her tiny suggestions of which billboards to gaze upon – the ones that would make her feel less sure of her beauty, of her ambitions, of her place in the world.

'See how wonderfully thin she is!' he whispered in her right ear, and she would suck in her belly.

'What a beautiful smile!' he spoke softly into her left. Her tongue pushed against her teeth and she noticed that one of them jutted out just a little further than the others. For a moment she wondered whether it could be fixed.

He hinted at which groups to avoid, insinuating that surely they must be speaking about her.

'Did you see how they looked at you? How they turned away?'

Soon, out of habit, she began to notice these things for herself, leaving him very little work to do. Yet there were times when he saw things going the wrong way.

When Jeda was twelve, Aunty came to visit, her loud, irksome voice somehow eliciting joyous laughter from the young girl. When she began talking about Rahami, he saw a change come over the child. Her eyes grew misty as she listened to Aunty speak of her mother. Of Rahami's annoyance at being caught at the airport with a suitcase full of dried fish and having to throw it away.

'Your mother was heartbroken. Like throwing a bag of gold in the rubbish!' Aunty laughed, the gap between her front teeth proudly exposed. 'And, daughter, the way she blasted me for feeding you porridge when you were just a baby. I told her, "A weaning baby that does not cry aloud will die on its mother's back!" Daughter, the noise you were making! She knew I was right . . . and look how strong you have become!'

Aunty was in full flow, regaling Jeda with all kinds of stories, her eyes bright and shining.

The Shadowman didn't like this. The girl was listening, and smiling. The cracks were thinning.

He slithered behind the wall and pushed a large daddy-long-legs into the light. It peered around, then quickly moved its long, spindly shape, scuttling back to the safety of darkness. Jeda was distracted by the creature.

'Aunty, did you see that?' she gasped, pointing at the wall.

Aunty heaved herself round, but there was nothing to see.

'See what?'

Jeda shook her head. 'Nothing, I guess.'

The spell was broken. The conversation ended. Aunty stood, stroked Jeda's face and embraced her tightly. As the door closed behind her, the Shadowman settled down. For him, it was safe again. For the time being. He would have to be careful. Some people were dangerous.

RAHAMI AND
A NEW WORLD

It is commonly known that death is the most absolute thing in the world. Even though it may arrive at an altogether inconvenient time, it will most certainly arrive. Rahami, Jeda's mother, had never considered the possibility that it would happen to her. She was a young, beautiful woman. Beautiful because she was sure of herself. She walked with grace and poise. She moved through the cobbled streets, glancing upwards at the exquisite stone buildings, their spires, domes and turrets disappearing into the haar, that thick, magnificent fog that rolled in from the sea and hung low over the city. Wherever she walked, people turned to marvel at this woman whose skin glistened like the midnight sky. They noticed the thickness of her lips, the sway of her hips, the casual confidence she exuded with a flick of her wrist or a slight tilt of her head. She smiled, for despite the differences she knew she loved this place as much as the distant land of her childhood.

Rahami loved words. As she peered through the ghostlike haze she mouthed *haar*. She had learnt it from a talkative stranger eager to share the wonders of his city. She liked the sound of it. It rolled off her tongue so easily. It was soft and gentle.

She thought of the old stories she had heard of this place. Women accused of witchcraft and sentenced to death. Fresh bodies stolen from their graves and sold for the advancement of science. Murder, torture, incredible wickedness! She imagined that in this magnificent city many of these stories had likely taken place under the cloak of the haar. It lent an air of mystery to everything it touched. Quite perfect for committing a crime.

When she had first arrived, she had tried to fit in, changing her clothes to mirror the grey and the dark. After a few years she realised that even though she was now of this place, she would likely never be seen as fully belonging, and so she decided there was absolutely no need to blend in at all. This city was hers regardless, and so she returned to wearing the bright clothes that spoke to no era or trend. She danced as the buskers played, her body remembering steps from a different world but which matched the rhythms so perfectly. She laughed loudly in places where silence was expected, spoke her mind regardless of who was present.

One day, as she meandered through the streets, she was struck by the striking red stone exterior of an ancient building close to the city centre. Realising it was a portrait gallery, she walked in, keen to learn more about the people so greatly admired for having contributed to this great city. A young man with scruffy brown hair was looking around and was drawn to her inquisitive spirit. There was a curiosity about him that appealed to her. He was nervous and made a terrible joke. She laughed. He smiled and told her of some of the faces he recognised in the paintings. She seemed genuinely interested. He asked if he might take her out. When she agreed, he planned the perfect date, a slow meal and a walk on the beach.

As the sun set, he found her fingers enveloping his. She smiled, and as he gazed into her sparkling eyes he thought that she was perhaps the most beautiful person in the world. They spoke, sharing stories of their lives, their thoughts, their dreams, their ambitions. They agreed to meet the following day, and then the next. They spent increasingly more time together, and Rahami began to notice how the blue of his eyes reminded her of an ocean she once knew, many thousands of miles away. Her eyes followed the curve of his jaw, and when she noticed the thinness of his lips, she began to wonder if those thin lips knew what lips were supposed to do.

Those lips must have spun a web of sweet words around her, as soon the two of them were inseparable. A few years later her skin tingled and trembled as those thin lips sealed their marriage with a kiss and it was not long after they were blessed with a beautiful daughter. They named her Jendayi, for though her birth had been long and arduous, she had arrived safely with a sweet smile. As her grandmother's name had been Jendayi, which meant gratitude, it appeared to be a perfect fit.

A tiny girl with skin the colour of gold, the thick, full lips of her mother and the round wide eyes of her father. Jeda, for that is how she came to be known, was very much loved. She was a wanted child, and she knew it, for her parents did their best to fill her life with joy.

Jeda and her father would spend the days creating wonderful new things together, using glorious shades of colour and light to bring them to life, but in the evening her mother would fill her world with words. They would snuggle in close together, and Rahami would take a comb and braid her daughter's hair. She would reach back into her childhood, remembering the stories her father had told her. Stories of the hyena men and the snake women who disguised themselves as beautiful strangers, arriving in villages and tricking gullible young people into marrying them before stealing them away to their fate.

While Jeda had never travelled to the place of her mother's childhood, she knew it vividly through these stories. She heard of talking chickens, eagles with sparkling, vibrant feathers and a magic needle to whom the rainbow willingly surrendered her colours. Her eyes widened in wonder as she imagined the sheer power of the deities who hurled each other across the Universe: the Mother of Fish in her robes of blue, the awesome power of the deity of beauty and divinity whose yellow skirts flowed as she danced around the world. Time and time again Jeda would insist on hearing the tale of the old hunched woman who, tired of the sky weighing down on her shoul-

ders, furiously knocked it back up into the heavens with her walking stick, where it remained to this day.

But often Rahami would share the stories she had learnt in her new world.

'Tell me, Jeda,' she would begin, 'what would you do if you met a wolf in the woods?' Then she would weave her story, leaving the child spellbound.

The child grew up with stories of changelings and selkies, of the bogle, of the wandering poet who rode on a horse through the skies holding on to the fairy queen, wondering at the rivers of blood and tears below. She learned of the soldier forced to leave his loved one and how they would never again meet by the bonny, bonny banks of their beloved loch. She heard of princesses flinging their hair out of tall towers and children abandoned to the forest because there was not enough food for them to eat at home.

'Did the witch die?' Jeda asked, after hearing what happened following the discovery of a gingerbread house, but Rahami would extend the mystery and leave things unsaid. Fuelled by these stories, Jeda many a time imagined herself playing the roles of warrior, ruler and healer, her dreams being so intense she woke up exhausted. Other times, she lay there, awake, a silly smile plastered over her face.

'Sleep, precious one,' Rahami would say, as she gently kissed her daughter's cheek and stroked her hair before closing the bedroom door behind her. Years later, Jeda would remember these moments as perhaps the happiest times of her life.

•   •   •

How wonderful it would have been if everyone loved those stories as much as Rahami and Jeda, but that was not the case. Rahami's best friend was Aunty, a larger, more opulent version of herself. While Rahami was quiet, Aunty was loud. While Rahami was not overly keen on shopping, Aunty would often arrive laden with bags, exhausted but happy. While Rahami preferred the natural look, Aunty would deftly fold the fabric of richly coloured headwraps into magnificent shapes that framed her face perfectly. Her mascara was thick, her lips a bright red and her numerous handbags were filled with all kinds of interesting niceties.

'Aunty is coming, sweetheart!' her mother would say.

'You're going to Aunty's house!' said her father.

'Come, greet Aunty!' Aunty would exclaim as she threw her arms out wide to embrace Jeda. As a child, Jeda never knew her by any other name. The comforting smell of warm bread and cinnamon surrounded her.

Jeda sometimes had the feeling that if Aunty squeezed a little harder she would be sucked into her enormous bulk and disappear forever. But she loved Aunty. There was always something to eat whenever she was around. In fact, if there was no food available within five minutes of Aunty requesting some, she would become visibly annoyed. And if Jeda refused to sit and eat with her, out would come one of her famous sayings: 'Jeda, if someone eats alone, how can they discuss the taste of the food with others?'

Jeda never knew how to respond to that one, so she would always feel obliged to have a little something, even if it were just a bite.

While Aunty loved spouting words of wisdom, she was less keen on stories. It always began with a kissing of the teeth and a roll of the eyes. 'Why? Why do you insist on telling her this nonsense?' she would say to Rahami. 'She will start having crazy ideas.'

'Nothing wrong with crazy ideas!' Rahami would retort, and Jeda would feel a little wave of exhilaration, imagining her mother as David defeating the giant Goliath.

'Does she know of the Sermon on the Mount? Hmm? How He fed the five thousand? Be wary,' Aunty would warn, 'the road you are walking. Stories can be dangerous!'

'And that is why I am so lucky to have you. You tell her those stories. There are too many others I want to share,' Rahami would reply, before jumping up, kissing Aunty on the head and attending to something.

Aunty would inevitably raise her eyebrows, gesticulate wildly or furiously cross her arms. Jeda would always leave the room at this point, fearful of being drawn into a loud battle, but had she waited a few minutes she would have found them laughing loudly over some nonsense in the kitchen, chattering away in a language she did not understand.

FEAR COMES KNOCKING

When Jeda was still young, a great lethargy overcame her mother. When Rahami's energy failed to return, her husband asked to accompany her to the doctor. She resisted at first: 'Why bother doctors with little things when there are really sick people in the world?' But he insisted, so to appease him she agreed to meet Dr Harrison.

They arrived at the clinic and looked around. The room was orderly. The doctor was kind, asking all sorts of questions with sincerity, giving nothing away. Tests were arranged. When the results came back, it was then that Dr Harrison delivered her blow. It was a cowardly illness, the kind that hides in quiet places slowly destroying you, piece by piece. It started by sucking the energy from her bones. It moved on to steal her shimmer, turning the glorious blackness of her skin into a dull, ashen grey. Cloaked in invisibility, it teased the sparkle from her eyes.

At first Rahami tried to hide it, even deny it. She forced herself to smile, although the effort often exhausted her. It took her longer to walk from room to room. She joked how it was the first time she'd had such prominent cheekbones, but in truth she wished her weight would return. She grew weaker and weaker, and though she tried to will herself back into good health it took some time before she realised she might not make it after all.

Would she be there to comfort Jeda after her first broken heart, or muse with her about the idiocy and wonder of the world?

Then the fear set in. Not for where she might be going, but for what would be left behind. Who would take her place? Who *could* take her place? Aunty? Who would teach Jeda about putting cold cabbage leaves on tender breasts? The best position to ease the pain of her period? Who could teach her the difference between love and hope? Who would be there to insist she followed her heart, or give her understanding of who she was? Who would encourage her, support her, be there for her, protect her, guide her? Was her husband enough? Who? *Who?* Her mind whirred endlessly. How could she cram a lifetime of learning into just a few short months? There were things her daughter needed to know. Important things.

So the nature of her stories began to change. She introduced the Shadowman, who in one story appeared as a great cloud of dust. In another he was a slithering creature, and in yet another a beautiful, golden angel. She spoke of him time and time again, but Jeda was young and didn't understand these new stories.

'Mummy, I don't want this one!' she would plead. 'Can you tell me the story of the selkie princess, the one who sang to the fisherman?'

'I will, my darling. But first you need to hear this.'

She took the comb and slowly started to tease out the knots in Jeda's thick curls. Her fingers unscrewed the jar of thick green hair pomade, full of lanolin, castor oil and bergamot. Large red and white lettering proudly proclaimed: 'Prevents the breaking of dry ends, resulting in thick, luscious locks'.

She massaged it into her daughter's scalp, humming a soft, wordless lullaby, and then she spoke.

'A long time ago, the gods were bored. Their eyeballs were numb from the sameness of the Universe and so, to alleviate their boredom, they had two choices: to destroy or to create.'

Jeda giggled. 'Their eyeballs were numb!'

Her mother continued.

'The gods knew that while smashing, crushing and hurling the planets and stars was great fun, the satisfaction lasted just a few moments and then it was gone. But to create something new . . . *that* took patience, effort and creativity. It was more of a challenge. So they formed a new planet and flung it into the wasteland of the sky. They created the first humans out of stardust and the rays of the sun. Forbidden from attempting to reach Heaven, these humans could feel joy and anger, greed and kindness, and they amused the gods for thousands of years.'

'Were they just like humans now?' Jeda asked.

'I suppose so,' her mother replied. 'They lived. They died. They had children. Perhaps things were a little less interesting because there were no trees, no animals, no hills or valleys, just endless grassy plains. What did make them different is that when the people were struggling or needed help they weren't afraid to ask for it. If somebody from a neighbouring village approached, they were welcomed, for everyone was curious about where they may have come from, and in this way they learnt many things. If somebody had a thought that was different to those of everyone else, they weren't nervous about speaking it out loud, for the others would be respectful and listen intently. So I suppose they were more content. But back to our story . . .

'One day the rays of the sun passed close to the surface of the Earth. Too close. The rays were so intense the grassy plains turned from green to yellow in a matter of minutes. The people became unbearably hot and there was nowhere to shelter. They had never experienced such discomfort. They suffered and struggled and finally they begged the gods, "Please help us, please save us, we cannot take this any more."

'The gods listened. As the people lay feeble on the ground, preserving every ounce of energy, a thin crack appeared in the sky. It was unlike anything the people had ever witnessed before. Accompanied by a rich crackling, like lightning, it grew wider and wider. As the sky parted, the people saw a strange object being lowered to the Earth. A magnificent creation, a great trunk, as wide as several elephants standing side by side. It had long branches that reached out in all directions, each one bearing thousands of green leaves. Its roots were like fingers and, as it touched the ground, they sank deeper and deeper until the tree – for that is what it was – stood firm. The people gazed in wonder upon it.'

'I bet it was the baobab,' interrupted Jeda.

Her mother smiled. 'It was. It was the mighty baobab! The Tree of Life. It was sent to help the people, its thick foliage shielding their delicate skin from the burning rays of the sun.

'The villagers raced towards it, sighing with relief as they flung themselves into the shade. However, their joy did not last, for the following day the sun rose with such fury it blackened the earth. The people could barely breathe. The shade of the leaves was simply not enough. They fell to the ground, their arms raised up to the heavens. "Please help us, please save us. We cannot take this any more."

'The gods listened. A silver sliver appeared in the sky. It slowly parted, revealing a lake of crystal clear water that sparkled and glittered as it floated down to the Earth. At first they were unsure of what to do – this was new to them. But soon they realised how cool and fresh the water was. Again, the people raced towards it. They dived in, flinging water over themselves and each other. The joy, sheer joy! They yelled with wild abandon, feeling free of all pain and misery. They sang. They rejoiced. All except for one man. His name was Ariké and he sat under the Tree of Life, his eyes narrowed, watching the others frolic in the water. He chewed his lip as he stroked his chin with his long, thin fingers. "We have nothing in this world," he mused to himself, "and yet in two days the gods have gifted us this magnificent Tree of Life and this beautiful lake. I wonder what else can be found in Heaven. There must be more."'

'How will he find out?' Jeda whispered, fearful of the answer.

'He took his axe and walked towards the tree.'

'No. Not the Tree of Life!'

'He raised the axe high into the sky . . .'

'But isn't it forbidden?'

'He brought it down, THWACK, and began to cut into the Tree of Life.'

'No!'

'Yes!'

'No!'

'He cut and cut until he had amassed a huge number of sticks.

Then he bound them together and started to build a ladder that reached up into the sky.'

'Didn't anyone try to stop him?'

'Oh yes, of course. Many of the people were angry. They knew they were not allowed to try and reach Heaven. They knew the gods may punish them. They pleaded with Ariké to come down. Do you think he listened?'

'No!'

'No, he did not. You see, Jeda, there were others who were curious to see what else could be found in the skies. When they saw the work involved, they did not want to make the journey themselves, but they were happy for Ariké to go first and encouraged him to climb. So he did. Higher and higher, until he arrived.

'When he first laid eyes on the home of the gods, it was beyond anything that he could have imagined. The colours. The fragrances. He saw strange beings walking around on four legs, many covered with fur, some with horns and hooves, others with claws and whiskers. He saw strange, winged creatures flying above his head. He held out a finger, gnarled and bruised from having worked so hard over the last few days, and remarked with wonder at the fragility and lightness of the delicate blue being that landed on his knuckle, its fluttering wings pulsing softly before launching itself once more into the sky.

'His eyes greedily took in the shapes, the curves and angles of this new world. The awesome mountains to the left whose white peaks disappeared into clouds of pink, green and blue. The valleys to the right, where trees similar to and very different from the Tree of Life grew together in harmony. The beguiling, hauntingly

beautiful babbling brooks, chirrups and tweets. The wind, dancing with the leaves, created harmonies that made his heart soar. There was nothing like this in his world. However, his presence had not gone unnoticed.'

'Oh, the gods must have been mad!' Jeda declared.

'They were furious with this man! How dare he? After everything they had given him. They glared at him. That simple look on his face. That disgustingly primitive mind, experiencing such intense beauty for the first time. He was a simple man who had dared to break their laws. There was no way around it. He had to be punished.'

'I think they may cut off his head!' Jeda volunteered.

'Is that what you would do?'

'That, or maybe they will throw him to the wild animals.'

'Ooh, that would be cruel!' Rahami responded, poking Jeda in the ribs. 'Actually, they came up with something a bit more interesting than that.'

'Oh? What did they do?' Jeda asked with eagerness.

'They decided to test him. They summoned him and took on their human forms as he approached. He looked around and saw billowing robes of every shade, the rainbow skirts, gold and ebony bracelets, silver jewellery that cradled cowrie shells, malachite, stones the colour of the sky, and more. The gods glistened. They shimmered. They shone. Ariké walked carefully and respectfully, wondering what they would do with him. He had broken the law and he knew there would be consequences. However, he also understood the gods to be fair and was ready to accept whatever would come his way.

'"Do you like what you see?" asked the God of Thunder.

'"It is beautiful," Ariké replied.

'"Do you wish for this in your world?" asked the God of the Harvest.

'"With all my heart," came his answer.

'"How would these gifts be received?" questioned the god who stands at the fork in the road.

'"We will fall to our knees, raise our arms to the sky and sing your praises forever," Ariké said with sincerity.

'A voice, soft as the wind, spoke next. "Then you will take whatever you wish back down with you. It is all yours."'

Jeda was confused. 'What? Aren't they going to punish him? It sounds like they are rewarding him!'

'Let the story unfold,' her mother replied.

'Ariké took the mountains and lowered them to Earth. He asked for the waterfalls, the rivers, the oceans, and he received them all. Next came the beasts of the land and the birds of the air; swarms of bees and butterflies flew past his ears and into the world. He pointed to the forests, bushes and flowers. He even asked for a stool made of pure gold that he eventually gifted to the Chiefs in the West, but what happened to that is a whole other story. He took everything he could see until he could not imagine asking for anything else. He had placed one foot on the topmost rung of the ladder, ready to make his descent, when another voice spoke.

'"These gifts are for the people, but this one here is just for you." The God of Wisdom handed Ariké a small calabash. A strong leather thong was threaded through a small hole, the loop large enough so that it would pass over his head and hang from his neck.

'"Ariké," the God warned, "you have broken one of our laws.

This is your chance to redeem yourself and prove your loyalty. Take this calabash as a parting gift, but only on the condition that you must never open it.'"

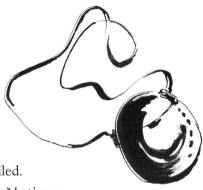

'I bet he opens it!' piped up Jeda.

'Really?' Her mother smiled. 'Would you disobey the gods twice? Let's see if you are right.'

'Ariké thanked the gods and wondered at such a request. Open the calabash! Why would he ever want to do that? He had everything he wanted. When he returned to his world and the people saw what he had brought them, why, he would be worshipped as if he were one of the gods himself. He would be adored. They would love him. They would give him everything he wanted. He had no need of anything else. And so, he accepted the calabash.'

•   •   •

Jeda didn't know what to think.

'Is it a trick?' she asked her mother.

'It may seem like it,' Rahami said quietly. 'But the gods do not trick with malicious intent. They are not deceitful, even though they sometimes test us in uncomfortable ways.

'Before his feet touched the ground, the celebrations had already begun. The people were desperate to see Ariké. To be close to him. To touch him. To celebrate him. He flung himself off the ladder into the loving arms of the awaiting throng. They chanted and cheered, as they carried him from village to village, the gifts from the skies finding their new homes on Earth.

'The crowds ululated, with clapping hands and stamping feet. Those who had rhythm and vibration played the newly gifted drums with abandon, the frenzied beat ensuring that nobody could stay still for long. They danced wildly, arms circling, hips gyrating, pure joy emanating from every pore. The feasting, the drinking, the dancing, the merrymaking lasted long into the night. It continued the following day and the day after that. For weeks they celebrated and Ariké was at the centre of it all.

'However, my darling . . .' Jeda's mother cuddled her. 'Humans are funny creatures.

'After just a few short months, the people had become used to all the things that Ariké had given to them. They no longer stared in wonder at the mountains as they kissed the clouds. They no longer marvelled at the sight of four-legged creatures mooing and braying as they grazed the fields around them. The children took it for granted that the giant rock from which they leapt into the plunge pool would always be there. Soon, Ariké received less attention. They no longer revered him. While they showed him respect and a few loyal neighbours occasionally brought him gifts, Ariké's status began to change and before long he became an ordinary man again.

'It didn't take long for him to realise how much he missed the adoration, how much he longed for them to call out his name. He craved it. His desire for it grew and grew, and slowly his attention turned towards the calabash around his neck. He began to wonder what could possibly be inside. At first, he tried to push the thought out of his head. He had disobeyed the gods once before and he dare not disobey them again. However, the more he thought about it, the more he convinced himself that the contents of the calabash must surely be extraordinary and his curiosity began to consume him. He couldn't eat. He could barely sleep. He took the calabash from around his neck, dug a hole, placed it inside and tried his hardest to forget about it. But it was impossible. He couldn't resist.'

'Oh no! Please don't open it. Please don't open it!' Jeda begged, as she clung to her mother.

'His heart was racing. Sweat poured down his face, as days later he pulled the calabash out of the hole and cradled it in his hand. He placed it close to his ear and shook it, as if that act would give some indication as to what magnificence lay inside. It gave nothing away. He looked around and watched the people going about their daily business with no thought of him whatsoever. This annoyed him. The feeling grated under his skin, so he walked over to the Tree of Life and placed the calabash on the ground below. He took his axe, the same axe that had cut down the tree's magnificent branches. He raised it above his head and, CRACK, he brought it down.

'The sharp blade smashed the calabash shell, which burst open, tiny splinters flying in all directions, and from within a thick, dark, grey shadow emerged. Ariké stared at it. It stared back. Then, slowly, small pieces began to break away and slither off across the dry earth in all directions, a swarming sea of sinister shadowy droplets.

'One made its way towards him. *What a curious thing*, Ariké thought to himself. It reached his leg and began to climb. "This is unpleasant," he murmured, as he tried to peel it off. The shadow stretched itself out, like a supernatural slug, and slowly began to

extend itself, winding around his torso, continuing its journey upwards, higher and higher, until it reached his ear, and then slowly, deliberately, it slipped its way in.'

There was a pause.

'And then what?' Jeda whispered.

'His eyes blackened. His body tingled. He looked up and felt a strange, unfamiliar sensation overcome him as he watched a figure descend from the ladder. He did not know it then, but she was the Goddess of Compassion. Her ebony skin glinted in the sunlight, her blue robes, the colour of the sky, billowing around her, her black eyes reflecting the gold of the beads that adorned her intricately styled hair. Ariké was confused. Once he would have stared at her with curiosity, but she was new to his eyes and now he was filled with a strange anxiety. His palms sweated, his throat was dry. He held his axe out in front of him in an attempt to keep her from him. She slowly reached out her long fingers towards him and called him by his name.

'"Ariké." Her voice was rich and full of kindness. The axe dropped, as he fell to his knees. He felt sick at the thought of what he had done and undeserving of any goodness shown to him. He wanted her to punish him. But what if she didn't? Would that be worse? Could he live with his guilt? These thoughts were exhausting. His breath came in short gasps. "What have I brought into this world?" he asked.

'"Fear," she replied softly.

'"Fear?"

'"It destroys the trust you have with the world and yourself."

'"I don't understand," he cried.

'"It is a little death that hides inside you. It may appear to protect you, but in truth it seeks to destroy what is most precious to you, and you may not realise what that is until it is too late."

'"Can you take it back?"

'"No."

'Ariké started to cry. "What can I do?" he mouthed, as his voice cracked.

'The Goddess of Compassion knelt by his side and stroked his head. "Tell the others. Make them aware of it. If they know it is there, they can choose not to listen to it."

'The Goddess of Compassion then slowly climbed the ladder, pulling it up behind her so that nobody else could ever make that journey.'

Jeda paused before asking, 'What happened to Ariké?'

'They say that he still wanders the Earth letting people know.'

'Why? Wait! You mean it is still in the world?'

Her mother stroked her head and looked up at the ceiling, then gently spoke. 'You need to know, Jeda, that the Shadow is everywhere. You, too, need to be aware.'

Jeda scowled, as she pondered her mother's words. Her mind was racing. She had so many questions, but when she turned to ask them she saw that her mother had fallen asleep and, not long after, Jeda slept too.

THE FILLING OF THE BOX

Rahami's treatment happened in cycles. For the first few days after she returned home from the hospital, she would race to the bathroom, kneel over the toilet bowl and retch violently. Jeda couldn't understand why something that was supposed to fix her would first have to make her so ill.

'It's a very strong medicine,' her father explained.

'But it is making her even more sick,' Jeda tried to tell him, as it was clear to her that he couldn't see.

'The thing that is making your mum ill is really powerful, so the medicine to cure her has to be strong enough to destroy it.'

'Yes,' her mother had added. 'I'll get used to it. I'll be fine. I promise.'

That was when the first lie was told. She lied time and time again after that. That she thought Jeda's specially made cookies, of which she only had one tiny bite, tasted delicious. That she was feeling better. How it wouldn't be long before she was back to herself again. She kept on lying until she was too weak to continue the lie. Too exhausted to keep believing them herself. In too much pain to want them to be true. And yet she needed to keep on.

The day before they planned to take her to the place where the health workers could better 'manage her needs', Rahami felt the walls shift around her and heard the old, familiar murmur of the Shadowman. It was time to keep her stories safe.

She understood their power and how, once released, they could not be kept silent. The Shadowman understood this power, too, and suspecting Rahami was up to something he could not control he watched, agitated. She could barely raise herself up into a sitting position, but she persisted. She reached for the little wooden box that sat waiting on the bedside cabinet. It was of a simple design, with a thin gold band running along the side. Some might have called it an insignificant box, but it was the only thing she had of her mother's and it was one of her most loved possessions. She opened the lid and began to speak her words. The stories tumbled out between dry, cracked lips. They forced themselves through in rasping whispers. They begged to be released, kept alive until they were needed again.

'Tell me, release me, please don't let me be forgotten,' they beseeched.

She poured them in. Myths, legends, histories, memories, ideas, languages, folk tales, every last one. She unleashed them all, and when she could not tell any more she closed the box and fell backwards onto the bed wheezing, desperate for breath. A few moments later Jeda entered the room, followed by her father and Aunty. Rahami gazed at her daughter, who approached cautiously, not wanting to disturb or cause her mother pain. Rahami beckoned her forward, then slowly gifted her the box. The girl took it.

'There will come a time when you will need this.' Rahami's voice

quivered as she spoke. She wanted to say more, but at that moment she saw Death enter the room. He approached her slowly, gently. Tears filling her eyes, she pleaded silently for just a little more time.

Death took pity on the woman and stepped back. Rahami held Jeda's head to her chest and began to stroke her hair. With every ounce of energy she murmured one of her favourite tunes, each word barely audible.

'You take the high road and I'll take the low road

'And I'll be in Heaven before you.

'You are my true love and we will meet again

'On the bonny, bonny banks of . . .'

And she was gone.

·　　·　　·

Over the next few years, Jeda grew into a charming young girl. She was polite, hardworking, always did as she was told. She was easy-going, never one to make a scene, liked to keep out of trouble. She found it difficult to make decisions, preferring to go with the flow.

'So, what would you like to do this weekend?' her father would ask, as they sat down for dinner.

'I don't mind,' she would answer, sweetly and sincerely. And so her father decided where they went and what they did. They enjoyed walks, they played tennis, they drank hot chocolate in cafes, they visited museums. She had once asked if they might go to the theatre, but her father had removed himself from this pleasure following the death of his wife. The stories that had once given him hope had lost his trust. He wanted to make his daughter happy and so looked into it, but the memories were still too raw and he told her perhaps they might catch some of the street shows instead. She never asked again.

It wasn't that Jeda didn't want to try new things or go to new places. She loved her father and deep down she was convinced that his happiness was often dependent on her sacrificing her own. Yet, had she reflected deeper, she would have understood that demanding more from her father, even though it may have annoyed him at times, would have instilled in him an even greater joy, because the truth was, he was happiest when she was too.

Jeda truly wanted to be, believed herself to be, a good person. She felt that always putting others first was the best way to accomplish that goal. Even though she struggled to state what she wanted, she knew that being good was important enough to outweigh all other things. However, she was often conflicted, as being good did not stop bad things happening to her. This shaky foundation gave the Shadowman immense pleasure, as it made his work even easier. Control was so much simpler when the individual wasn't quite sure of themself.

It started off with little things designed to strip away at her confidence. When she first started high school, he made sure she encountered her main source of consternation, a malicious, desperately unhappy sprite disguised as a smart, popular girl with golden hair and eyes the colour of sapphires. It's greatest joy was to drag others down.

'I suppose if you can't get attention from your mother, you need to get it at school,' it sneered, after Jeda had received rapturous praise from a teacher.

Jeda tried to ignore the whiny voice but found her fists clenching uncontrollably.

'Shut up, idiot,' came a voice behind her. Jeda turned to see an unlikely ally. Standing a full head shorter than Jeda, he was known for being one of the most troublesome kids in the school.

'Now I've seen it all,' the sprite smirked. 'The psycho and the monkey. Defending your girlfriend?'

'Don't speak about my mother!' Jeda trembled as she spoke, her nostrils flaring with rage.

The sprite leaned back and howled with laughter. 'Admitting your mother's a monkey now?' The sprite's team of supporters stood giggling in solidarity. The boy stepped forward to offer support, but Jeda pushed him away.

She sniffed but too late. A strand of silver snot dripped from Jeda's nose.

The sprite recoiled, grimacing.

'Gross!'

As Jeda quickly wiped it away with the back of her hand, the sprite leaned forward and whispered, quiet enough so nobody else could hear, 'If I had an ugly, stupid, snotty kid like you, I would have chosen to die too!'

The punch was fast, knocking the sprite to the ground before it had a chance to react. It lay there wailing, blood pouring from its nose.

'She hit me! She broke my nose!'

The adrenaline coursed through Jeda's veins, making her tremble. The group of excited school children piled over each other, each one eager to see the latest goings-on. One yell from the on-duty teacher forced them to scatter, and moments later both Jeda and the sprite found themselves seated in the headteacher's office. Jeda was in no mood to speak. The scowl on her face told its own story, as she watched the sprite whimpering pathetically, holding a damp cloth against its perfect nose.

'This isn't like you at all. You're not a troublemaker,' the headteacher remarked, facing Jeda. When he pressed her on why the incident had taken place, Jeda couldn't tell him. He issued a stern warning that if it ever happened again he would have no choice but to expel her.

Jeda wished he would do it now, so she would never have to go back to school again.

Her father was well aware of the situation and by the time she reached home he was ready for her. He paced back and forth, waving his hands hysterically, his voice full of bitter disappointment.

'I expected better from you. I really did.'

They were both so angry they did not notice the Shadowman watching every move, rubbing his hands with glee. A perfect opportunity had arisen. When she was sent to her room, she slammed the door in anger and screamed into her pillow, outraged at how unfair life was. She hated her father. He could never understand. She wished her mother was there.

The Shadow flitted softly around Jeda and began to whisper so quietly that it was easy for her to believe that it came from inside her own head.

'You have made quite a lot of mistakes,' the Shadowman suggested, ever so gently. 'One or two might have been understandable. Perhaps she was right about the other things, too?'

Jeda paused and considered this idea. Maybe her mother did think she was ugly. She knew she definitely was not the smartest kid in school. She could hear the sprite's words all over again. 'Yes, possibly,' she agreed, then she flung her head into her pillow and wept.

The Shadowman grinned.

For the next few years, he was her constant companion.

·   ·   ·

It would be fair to say that Jeda did not like school. It was tedious and she often felt a great weight on her shoulders when she was expected to understand things of which she had no knowledge whatsoever.

Her history teacher was the worst. He may have liked Jeda. He may not have meant her any harm. Yet he alienated her by constantly seeking her opinion on topics where he felt she should excel.

'Jeda,' came the dreaded voice, 'you must know what the runaway slaves were called.'

She did not, and swallowed hard, hot waves flooding over her.

'I'm sure Jeda could tell us,' he informed the class brightly when they discussed how best to refer to darker-skinned members of the population. Jeda had no idea and wished the ground would swallow her up. Every night she prayed that she could become invisible. And, as though helping her wish to come true, she began to withdraw from her social circle, preferring the company of television characters who did not ask difficult questions, or expect her to behave in a certain way. The troubled individuals allowed her to escape the torments of her own pathetic existence and she immersed herself in shows that promised only happiness and joy.

She enjoyed her own company, and took great pleasure in drawing and sketching objects that she found of interest: trees, imaginary creatures, clouds that took on strange and unusual shapes. Her father had flung himself into his work, spending long days and nights immersed in it, and so he encouraged this skill, as it was the only glimpse he had into her world. But Jeda knew that he could never truly appreciate what she was going through. Nobody could.

School had just closed for the Easter holidays and Jeda was on her way home. She was thrilled that for the next few weeks she would finally have some respite and be free to do whatever she wished. She was lost in thought when the bus passed a large public park with a natural pond. Jeda's head was resting on the glass window and she gazed at the excitable ducks eagerly diving for the peas and bread thrown in by passers-by.

She had watched this scene unfold hundreds of times before, but on this occasion she remembered the day her mother had taken her there and an enormous swan had lunged at her, hissing loudly. She had been terrified and stood rooted to the spot, but her mother snatched her up and carried her to safety. She had not thought of it in so many years, yet today it was as clear as though it had happened yesterday. The memory triggered another, then another, each one so vivid that when she finally arrived home she headed straight to her room, reached under her bed and, just as she had done so many times before, she pulled out the box.

She sat on her bed, the unassuming wooden container resting on her knee. The latch was a simple hook but, just like the previous times, Jeda couldn't bring herself to loosen it. She wasn't thinking

of anything in particular when suddenly a loud knock at the door alerted her to her senses. Annoyed at having been disturbed, she scowled, then got up and went to open it. Standing on the doorstep was Aunty, a stern look on her face.

'Aunty!' Jeda began, shocked.

She didn't get much further, as Aunty swept past her and proceeded to hang her coat up in the hallway. She slipped off her expensive-looking high-heeled shoes, took out a pair of fluffy gold slippers from her bag, placed them on her feet, then made her way through to the kitchen. Jeda sighed as she closed the front door and sheepishly followed her through, anticipating a thorough dressing-down. She had not spoken to Aunty in weeks and she realised that perhaps she had ignored a few too many messages.

Aunty sat down expectantly at the table. Jeda meekly placed the box down, then proceeded to put the kettle on. The two sat in silence as the whistle of steam carried through the room. Once the tea had been made and poured out, Aunty slowly stirred hers round and round. The entire time her eyes never left Jeda. Finally, she took a long, slow sip, then placed the cup on the table.

'Daughter!' For that was how she referred to Jeda. 'You think I have not been watching?'

There was a great pause.

'Look at your hair. You have changed.'

Jeda nervously stroked her smooth, silky hair, straightened to within an inch of its life.

'Look at your body.'

Aunty moved her hands in delicate royal waves, as though imagining the curves that had once graced the girl. Jeda swallowed hard and noticed that perhaps her shoulders were a little more hunched than was necessary, maybe she had skipped a few too many meals. To her great annoyance, her stomach rumbled at that precise moment.

Aunty stood up sharply and proceeded to walk around the poor girl. As though trapped inside some magic circle, Jeda felt unable to move. Aunty sat back down and examined Jeda further, her face like stone, then she flung her arms forward.

'Where is your fire?' Her frustration was clear. 'You have changed! You are a lion trying to be a cat.'

Jeda was uncomfortable in a way she hadn't been in a long time. The voice continued, punctuated with wild gesticulations, becoming louder, fiercer, almost angry. The knot in Jeda's stomach tightened. She was filled with hot rage. Aunty clearly did not understand how difficult things were for her. How could she?

'Yes, this is your home. But you have another home across the oceans and among the stars, yet you squeeze yourself into a tiny hole. You are more than you know. Your mother knew that. You know that!'

Jeda's nostrils flared as she tried to control her breathing. She wanted to scream, to tell Aunty that she didn't want another home. She was glad she didn't live in some nasty, poor village. She knew exactly what it was like. She had seen the pictures where everyone was hungry and flies crawled over lips, eyes and noses. She had a perfectly good home and she was happier than she had ever been. But as she racked her brain for the words she wanted to say, Aunty's eyes suddenly noticed the box that Jeda had laid on the table. Her expression softened, her shoulders relaxed and there was a firm yet gentle look in her eyes as she patted it softly.

'Open the box, but only when you are ready to listen.'

Once Aunty had left, Jeda seized the box and angrily shoved it under her bed, as though doing so would rid her of Aunty's presence. She stormed to the bathroom and washed her face. Her hands gripped the sink, as she gazed into the mirror. She saw her mother's nose and lips, the arched eyebrows. Although the thought annoyed her, she began to feel that perhaps there was some truth in what Aunty had said – but as soon as the thought entered her head, the voices began. It was the Shadowman.

Trying desperately to undo the damage that had been done, he glowered back at Jeda through the mirror. 'How dare Aunty speak such nonsense! You know exactly who you are. You know you are strong.' Having cast doubt on Aunty's words, the Shadowman focused his attention on Jeda's suffering. 'You have done so much, put up with so much. You can handle anything the world throws at you.'

Memories immediately began to fill Jeda's mind. She had been through a lot. Her mother's death. Her father's absence. He had immersed himself in work and only appeared when he would pop his head round the door to wish his daughter a goodnight. There was Aunty's constant prying, the incessant pressure to behave a certain way at school, her ugliness, the endless reminders of what a failure she was, how she simply didn't fit in anywhere . . . The walls around her began to heave. It was too much. She needed to get out. She raced through the front door and ran to the nearby park, hugging her coat to her.

The cold air flowed freely around her face as she inhaled deeply. It felt good. As she moved, she noticed a small group of teenagers sitting on a park bench. She recognised one immediately and lowered her gaze, hoping to pass by undetected.

'Well, well. Look who's come to join us!' the sprite's tormenting voice rang out, grating and unwelcome as it flicked its golden, shiny hair over its shoulder.

Jeda ignored it and continued walking.

'Ooh! Think you're too good for us, do you?'

Jeda wondered whether she should turn around and go home, but to do that was to admit that she was scared. She was, but she certainly didn't want them to know. She dug her hands deeper into her pockets, lowered her hood and continued walking. Had they just let her be, she wouldn't have found herself where she did, but they simply could not leave her alone.

'Ooh, no friends today?'

'Not with that hair!'

'Ugly bitch mother, ugly bitch daughter.'

At first the words stung like pinpricks, but soon they pierced deeper. Like steel barbs they took hold, designed to wound and cause pain. She tried to protect herself but the words were too sharp. She realised she was not as strong as she thought she was. Her mother was no longer there to protect her. She was alone.

The tears welled up instantly.

Jeda started to run.

'Jeda!'

She heard a voice calling her name. She followed it, racing across the park, through the streets, oblivious to the furious beeping of horns as cars braked sharply to avoid her.

'Jeda!'

She sped towards the old town, fast over the cobblestones, down the tiny closes. The glorious turrets of the nearby palace went unnoticed as she headed for the mountain and started to climb. The city took on its familiar grey. Weighty clouds hung overhead, determined to block out any warmth from the sun. The crags stood silent and brooding, unmoved by her sorrow. She did not feel the wind on her face or notice the stones crumbling beneath her feet.

'Jeda!'

She scrambled higher and higher, chasing the voice that seemed to promise a way to end the roaring sound in her ears. Tears flowed down her cheeks. She wiped them away and continued to climb. As she neared the top, she looked out on a scene she knew well. The ugliness she felt inside was too great, preventing her from seeing the beauty that lay before her. The ancient castle on a hill, the glittering water in the distance.

'See how it sparkles like a thousand arrowheads,' her mother had once said to her.

Machines tearing down old worlds and building new. But now, the only sound she heard was the jumbled murmuring of ghostly voices, those who had helped build this land and, for whatever reason, had not been able to move on. The voices were all-consuming, speaking of blood and gold, blood and gold.

'Jeda.'

One voice cut through the others.

For a moment, she saw thick, red blood seeping through the soil, bubbling to the surface. It quickly began to pool and, as it grew into a mass of water, she saw figures reaching out, waiting for her to save them.

She screamed and scrambled upwards.

'Jeda.' The voice urged her on. She continued her ascent. She reached the top of the mountain and saw a cairn of stones before her. There, a figure stood silent and still, as though waiting. She approached slowly. It did not move.

'Who are you?' she cried.

Silence.

Around her the clouds gathered, dark and brooding. The figure stood watching. She drew closer.

Then suddenly the figure stepped forward and gazed upon her.

A cold chill ran over her. As he moved, he glittered like a million stars on a winter night, his brilliance so intense she raised an arm to shield her eyes.

'Is this better?' His voice was soft. Jeda felt his fingers wrap themselves around her arm, lowering it to her waist. Gone was the piercing light and in its place was a shadowy form. She reached out to touch him, but his skin dissolved into nothing, as though he were dust. She was drawn to him. He was so familiar. She looked up, but where his eyes should have been Jeda saw nothing but swirling black pools. She closed her eyes and imagined this was death. She waited, prepared to accept whatever was to come her way. She felt his shadowy fingers caress her cheek, his hand on her waist as he circled around her.

His voice was so clear, as he whispered in her ear.

'I see that you are lonely. I can see your pain.'

She gasped.

He could see her!

'I see that you're tired. As though it's all in vain.'

He understood her.

She began to sob unashamedly.

'I can help you. Take it all away. I can help you. Give you a gift today.'

He stroked her hair so gently. He moved to her other ear, as a lover might do, and spoke, stretching out each word.

'All I ask is one tiny thing.'

Anything.

She would do anything.

'Just bring me the box and you will feel nothing.'

She opened her eyes and silently promised him what he wanted and more. He smiled, then, gently holding her face in his hands, he leaned forward and kissed the gift of emptiness into her. She accepted. The kiss was so soft that she did not notice his dark cloud-like form slip down her throat, into her chest, find the cracks and settle in.

She did not know how long she had been standing there, but when she opened her eyes the colours around her were a little less bright, the sharp wind did not sting her skin, her ears barely noticed the sweet birdsong. She walked slowly back to her house, went up to her room and reached under her bed for the box.

A STORY IS UNLEASHED

Once more the box lay in her hands. Jeda had often gazed at it, tracing her finger over the gold band before placing it back, declaring what a foolish thing it was, unaware of the importance of what it contained. But this time it felt different. She remembered afresh the pain etched on her mother's face as she had reached over for the box all those years ago.

'There will come a time when you will need this,' Rahami had rasped before the effort became too much and she had collapsed back on the bed.

Inside Jeda the Shadowman shifted.

'It is nothing. Just a few old memories. They are holding you back. You must destroy it!' he urged.

She slowly stood, ready to take the box wherever she was told, to pretend it had never existed at all.

'That's it!' he crowed gleefully. 'No need for such ridiculous things.'

Her eyes glazed over, and she was in such a state that she was not aware of the front door opening. She did not detect the faint odour of cinnamon in the air, or notice Aunty's footsteps coming up the stairs. She certainly did not hear Aunty's voice as she hesitantly tried to find the words to make peace.

'Daughter, if we cannot solve our problems in peace, how can we solve them in war? Come, let us talk.'

Sensing trouble, the Shadowman leapt into action.

'Move!' he screeched. Jeda reached for the door handle just as Aunty entered, knocking the box out of her hands. They both tried to grab it, as it tumbled towards the ground, twisting and turning as though filled with a life of its own. Jeda caught it just as it was about to hit the floor, but as she did the little hook on the side found its way loose and slipped out of the catch. Immediately a glow filled the room, the box became red hot, blistering Jeda's skin, and, gasping in pain, she dropped it to the ground.

'Noooo!' snarled the Shadowman.

But it was too late.

The lid had burst open, filling the room with a brilliant glow. Out flew story after story, swirling around Jeda's head like a dazzling swarm of tiny gold and silver bees. The Shadowman was incensed. Years of gaining control and now this! But, sensing the danger he was in, he took control of Jeda's body, raising her arm to protect himself. A tiny spark hit her fingers, sending a jolt of electricity through her body. A golden glow rushed through her veins as she felt the world spin around her. She found herself hurtling through time, an intense, almost painful buzzing in her ears, then it stopped and she was floating in a warm envelope of air. She closed her eyes, as she felt her mother's arms around her. Her voice was so sweet.

'Jeda. Jeda.'

And then Rahami began.

'A long time ago . . .'

Of course it would begin this way. Her mother's stories always did.

'A long time ago, there was once a powerful queen who ruled over a tiny nation . . .'

The warm air in which she felt so at peace released her without warning and Jeda found herself spat out onto a cold, hard surface. Around her, a thunderstorm was raging. She pulled herself up, but the wind tore at her. The rain lashed down as dark, angry clouds violently transformed themselves into wild and furious shapes. Her hair clung to her cheeks and she squinted hard, struggling to see anything in the dark. In the distance, lightning flashed and, to her horror, she saw a mighty wave racing towards her. Along with everything else in its path, she was caught up in its flow and as she tumbled round and round, struggling to find which way was up and which was down, she was plunged into a cold, grey sea. She gasped with shock, then swam to a nearby bank where she pulled herself out and fell back exhausted, her teeth chattering with the cold.

She lay there, stunned, for a few moments. Then it dawned on

her how blue the sky was. The thunderstorm was over, but she had no idea where she was. She stood up and was surprised to see her clothes and hair were completely dry. She looked around and saw that she was near a bustling port. Elaborately carved sailing ships were moored to the docks, with hundreds of men and women carrying, pushing, pulling and heaving great loads around her. Their clothes were dark and smeared with dirt, oil and spices, in sharp contrast to the robes worn by the lords and ladies who wandered by, arm in arm. Their beautiful coats and skirts had stitching so fine it was barely visible to the eye. Their colourful, polished boots clickety-clacked over the cobblestones as they headed, no doubt, to their fine townhouses. They swanned past Jeda, paying no attention to her at all. Around her the cries of market traders rang out: 'Come buy, come buy!' Stalls struggled to hold the weight of fresh fish,

warm bread and vegetables of all shapes and sizes.

Jeda noticed a young girl skipping too close to the gutters for her mother's liking. She was no older than seven or eight. Her mother grabbed her hand, pointed to the ground, then looked the girl in the eye.

'Your grandfather laid these stones. He worked late and he worked hard so that you could keep your shoes out of the mud. He did a great thing, your grandfather.'

Then, lifting up her hefty skirts, she marched them on. In that moment, Jeda realised she knew nothing about any of her grandparents. There had been snippets, but when her mother had tried to tell her she hadn't been interested. Those stories she had been told were now largely forgotten. She cursed herself, wishing that she had paid closer attention.

The sound of a fiddle and boisterous singing shook her from her contemplation. She followed the sound and peered through a doorway to see an audience enjoying the tunes played by three musicians. The fiddler's eyes were closed as his fingers worked their magic, whipping up the small crowd into a great frenzy. The flautist's eyes were wide open, relishing the adoration, and the accordion player was a girl with a pained expression on her face as she gave everything her soul had to offer. It was captivating. The audience cheered them on, singing loudly, several of them dancing round the tables. Jeda watched as their faces lit up with joy, when suddenly her mother's voice filled her ears.

'The nation was rich in stories and music and song, but for many of the people this great treasure was not enough. They longed for something more and because they couldn't find it in their homeland they decided to leave in search of it.'

The crowd disbanded when a large bearded man came charging into the room. 'How many times must I tell you! No dancing in your lunch break! We leave in a few hours. Get back to it.'

With sighs and a few coins tossed in a box, the audience headed to the exit, complimenting the entertainers on their way out. As they left, a loud trumpeting sound was heard and Jeda found herself pushed along the quay towards a great stage at the far end. She was crushed between the large bearded man and another slim, well-dressed character who appeared to be trembling with excitement.

On the stage, an exuberant character in gaudy attire was prancing about, announcing the imminent arrival of Her Majesty the Queen. The excitement was palpable. Suddenly the trumpets blew again, heralding her royal arrival. The jester stepped to the side as a large, bloated creature waddled onto the stage, accompanied by several ladies who flurried around her in a confusing manner. Everything about her was loud and ostentatious. Her frilly-neck collar stretched almost a metre around her, preventing her from moving freely. When she looked around at her audience expectantly, her movements seemed forced and unnatural. The people cheered and applauded loudly, and when the Queen was satisfied she began.

'Ladies and gentlemen, I am pleased that so many families have come out to give our brave adventurers such a fine send off. It is exciting to see what you will accomplish with your hard work. We are a great nation, but we can be greater. Remember, you may go where you will, take whatever you find, but return to the Queen what is deservedly hers.'

The Queen turned to one servant, who handed her a basket of gold coins. She reached in and, scooping out a few handfuls, she flung them into the crowd. She stood back and watched as even the best-dressed citizens clawed at the ground, their eyes wide in a desperate bid to seize just one piece of gold. One of the musicians noticed his son race forward to join the throng. He grabbed him by the scruff of the neck.

'Never like that, son. Let her hand it to you, looking you in the eye!'

The boy stood with his head high and proud next to his father. There was something regal about them, despite their patched clothes and holey shoes. Jeda found herself wishing that her father didn't have to work so hard. Maybe he didn't have to chase money all the time.

Jeda was distracted by the sound of yelling. With no more gold to be found, the crowd now dispersed, travellers eagerly clambering aboard their ships. Babbling voices, excited at the prospect of what lay ahead, filled the air. Some were seeking adventure, others an escape, many to satisfy their urge of possessing more gold.

Jeda looked back at the stage. There, she witnessed the insatiable Queen take handfuls of gold pieces, place them into her mouth, swallow them down, mop the edges of her lips with a silken hand-kerchief, then wobble her way down the quay towards the first moored ship.

'The ship's captain summoned the clouds down from the sky and reined them to the magnificent vessels with golden, billowing sails. Dressed in their finery, the passengers climbed aboard.' Rahami's voice echoed across the chaos. *'The Queen cut the ropes with a silver sword and the crowds gathered and cheered, waving off their loved ones as they set off for new worlds.'*

Jeda watched as the ships began to float off into the sky. She was seized with a desire to know where they would go, so she raced along the quay and leapt up, reaching for a rope that hung from a low passing vessel. She gripped on, as the ship climbed higher and higher, before pulling herself onboard. The crew were making plans to attempt new routes, some of which only existed in their stories. She was curious as to where they had heard these tales told, so when a young crewman came walking towards her, his fiery hair glistening in the sunlight, she decided to ask.

She smiled. He did not smile back. She waved her hand, but he gave no indication of warmth or interest. She decided to stand right in front of him and that was the moment she realised that he did not see her at all, for he walked right through her. She was a mere passer-by in someone else's story. She could change nothing, influence nothing, ask nothing. It was as though she simply didn't exist. The idea shocked her.

'And so, my darling,' her mother's voice returned, *'as they explored the skies, they looked down and saw an extraordinary land.'*

Jeda peered over the edge of the vessel and saw her mother was right. The rivers glittered with the clearest water, the mountains sparkled with diamonds that lay just below the surface. The valleys were filled with vibrant forests, and the plains showed the movement of strange and beautiful creatures. The ships anchored and the crew began their descent, dropping to the ground before the startled population who, adorned in magnificent attire, emerged to greet the newcomers.

'Just like in the land from which they had left, the people of this new land loved to sing. They adored music. They would stay awake long into the night telling stories around a crackling fire. It was their favourite time of the day. And they loved riddles too, Jeda, just like you.'

Jeda smiled as she remembered her parents scolding Aunty for giving her sweets in return for guessing the answers to riddles.

'Tell me, child,' Aunty had said, 'my house is perfect, but it has no door. Who am I?'

Jeda had puzzled for several moments before hesitantly piping up, 'An egg?'

Aunty had crowed with delight, scooped her up and told her how proud her ancestors would be, before issuing sweet treats in shiny wrappers.

Jeda gazed at the crowd before her and understood their delight, as each one sat absorbed in the words that brought them together.

'But while the explorers enjoyed themselves at these gatherings, they considered the first people rather simple and foolish. They did not see how the people of this land spoke to the trees and the wind. How they understood the clouds, who informed them that the rains were coming. How centuries had shaped their language into poetry. However, they loved the land and decided to settle. Follow the bearded man, Jeda.'

Jeda did as her mother's voice commanded and went after the ship's captain, as he was carried across the plains on an ornately carved palanquin held up by four strong men. He revelled in this unparalleled luxury, clicking his fingers, then asking a young boy to swat away insects. In his left hand, he held a flag. They walked on for some time, when, to the right of them, great, green hills loomed up, reminding him of home.

'Take me there!' he commanded.

They did as he requested.

At the foot of the hills, Jeda saw him leap down from his transport, bend his knees and crumble the rich, fertile earth in his fingers. He saw no fences or barriers, just a few homesteads, and to him it was clear that those who lived there neither valued nor understood how best to make use of this land. Deep inside him, he heard a small voice declare that he was infinitely more capable than those around him. He smiled and, with new eyes, realised what wonderful servants these people would make. He raised his flag high into the air and brought it down with a powerful thrust, breaking the earth and claiming it for himself and his Queen.

· · ·

Jeda watched as he and the others planted homes across the land. She saw how the roots grew thick, spreading far and wide, pushing the first people out of their homes. They complained at the injustice but were promised jobs to till the earth and grow what was asked of them. When they refused, the settlers unveiled a weapon more powerful than a club, a blade or a bullet. The most skilled warriors could take a word, twist it, mould it, shape it into a hard, cruel weapon and the right word could make an army lay down its guns or cause a man to hold a knife to his brother's throat.

The old laws of this new land were quickly disbanded and Jeda felt a shift in the atmosphere, almost overnight.

'Jeda, let me introduce you to a boy.'

Jeda caught sight of a skinny, scrawny child with bright, shining eyes. He worked for the bearded captain, carrying messages here and there, doing odd jobs around the compound. He was intrigued by the sight of the books around him and how their contents appeared to speak to the settlers. It amazed him that the books agreed to speak to the strangely dressed women who had arrived to settle with their men. He was fascinated that they had access to the secrets within, for this could never take place in his world. Over the next few days Jeda caught him sneaking peeks several times. He knew that the books contained great wisdom but he was frustrated – when he held them to his ear, they did not speak to him.

'Time to move, Jeda.' Rahami's voice carried on the wind.

Jeda followed the boy into a forest. She called after him, but he was nowhere to be seen.

For the first time in this new world, she felt fear.

SOMETHING HAS TO CHANGE

It was darker than a thousand nights, with the trees growing so close to each other the forest was almost impenetrable. Jeda's heart pounded in her chest. Then she saw a tiny chink of light. As she quickly made her way towards it, grateful to be out of the dark, she was quite unaware of the thorns and twigs piercing her skin. The trees began to thin and, before her, she saw a small village. Her eyes searched for the boy, but he was nowhere to be seen.

'Go to the first house, Jeda,' her mother's voice instructed.

Jeda peered in and saw a handsome young man with his wife, whose warm smile lit up the room. There was a tiny child in his arms: a girl with skin the colour of the midnight sky and eyes that shone brighter than a million stars.

'The boy became a man and a father. He had one daughter, his pride and joy. He had watched her grow from a tiny baby who gurgled happily – she had the most beautiful black eyes and soft wet lips – to a girl full of curiosity and interest in the world. The rest of his family laughed, stating that she should have been born a boy. You see, Jeda, in the village a boy grew to become a man with a trade or a skill, but a woman was a woman like a cow is a cow. She was to become a wife and a mother and that would be her destiny.

'But her father was watching his world change around him. He knew that words held power and could be woven into something with great strength, not just swept away on the wind. He wanted his daughter to learn these new ways and so he requested that one of the more approachable settlers teach her. It was a role the stranger relished to the discomfort of many. The father knew that there were those in his community who would struggle to accept this arrangement, aware of their fears that a young girl could have access to so much power. His suspicions were confirmed when he overheard his brothers talking in secret.

'"You know, he is teaching his daughter!"

'"Imagine if anyone finds out – the shame!"

'"Wasting his money on what? A girl! He is a fool!"

'"It is not his money that he wastes. It is our inheritance."

'There was silence for a moment.

'"What shall we do, brothers?"

'There was a longer silence, then the decision was made.

'The father knew it was no longer safe, so in the middle of the night, with the blessing of his wife, who could not leave her many other responsibilities, he took a small bag containing only food and water. He took his daughter by the hand and, without a backward glance, they left the only home they had ever known.'

Jeda followed, as the father walked for three nights. They came to a forest unlike any that Jeda had ever seen before. Many of the trees were so large that it would take twenty people to encircle them. They were tall and dark, their finger-like branches stretching up into the sky, but the forest glittered, it whispered, it beckoned. They walked in silence.

Jeda noticed that at no point did the father mark the trees. He had no intention of ever going home.

The young girl walked with purpose, trusting that her father would always do what was right by her. Just as Jeda was wondering whether she would have been so trusting, without warning the hairs on the back of her neck began to tingle. Her instincts sharpened as she saw a fine mist swirling around them. A familiar dread overcame her. She knew exactly who it was.

The Shadowman had sensed a growing power in the young girl and was determined to put an end to it. He would not allow her to believe that she had any sort of control over herself. Jeda needed to warn them.

'Run!' she cried. 'He is here!' But they heard nothing. She raced in front of them, waving her arms and shouting her warning, but it fell on deaf ears and they marched on, oblivious to her presence.

'Please let them hear me!' she begged, but to no avail.

They entered a clearing and the Shadowman swirled around the girl's feet. She stopped as he enveloped her, whispering into her ear, 'You are not strong enough for this. You are not brave enough.'

The girl's brow furrowed as she contemplated the words.

'Don't listen to him. Don't listen,' Jeda beseeched.

The Shadowman continued. 'You are just not smart enough.'

The father recognised the danger: he had heard those words himself many times before. He needed help and so he raised his arms, opened his throat and cried out, 'Upepo!'

A mighty wind rushed through the branches, swept up the man and his daughter, and carried them high above the trees. Jeda managed to leap up just in time. The father and daughter clung to each other, looking down as their beloved land – the glittering mountains, with the animals roaming free – rushed away from them. He held his daughter a little tighter and prayed that one day, just like the children he could still see splashing in the river, she could play freely too.

•   •   •

High above the land, the three sat in silence, contemplating their situation. The father gazed down at his daughter and began to sing a lullaby. Jeda found it vaguely familiar and was able to hum along. Soon the girl had fallen asleep. Her father stayed awake, vigilant. He would occasionally rest his head on his knees, but Jeda could see he was perplexed. She watched him stroke the child's hair when she murmured restlessly.

The next morning, as they travelled further on, the father noticed a fine mist sweeping across the hills and valleys. Just under the surface of the Earth he noticed the great roots, planted by the settlers and now spreading over swathes of land, pushing the original inhabitants into smaller and less fertile areas. He heard wails, as many mourned the loss of their ancestors' resting places, saw sacred trees being felled to make way for new homes. Skirmishes were taking place between his people and the settlers.

Jeda watched the father's stomach tighten when he saw great lines of men chained together, dragging themselves forward, as though an enormous creature with rotting limbs crawling reluctantly and painfully towards its nest. It was not long before a great stench filled his nostrils and belly, making him retch. Below them was the nest. Enormous camps where thousands and thousands of his people were held with no shade, no water, patrolling guards who lashed out with leather whips if someone coughed or uttered the wrong

word or simply because they dared look them in the eye. The barbed wire surrounding them glinted viciously in the sunlight, ready to rip and tear the flesh of those who dared dream of freedom. A tall gate with razor-sharp wire was the entrance to this hell and it creaked open to welcome its latest residents.

Jeda saw tears streaming down the face of the man as he watched the scene unfold. She wished she could offer him some comfort, some sense of hope. She understood how shocked he must be watching his people go through so much pain. It had to be the worst thing in the world.

Understanding Jeda's thoughts, Rahami reassured her.

'No, Jeda. It was not the stench of blood and sweat and pain that shocked the father most. It was not the screams of men rolled up in barbed wire or tortured with bottles, sand and scorpions. It was the fact that it was his own people who listened so intently to the words of the Shadowman, that they whipped and beat with such fury, such rage, such hate that their eyes glowed red. Around them all, the fine mist continued to swirl.'

Jeda cried out, 'Why am I here? Why do I need to see this?

'You will see.'

•   •   •

They continued on the wind.

Out of nowhere, the clanging of a great bell sounded. Below them was a beautiful walled garden full of flowering bushes, with bursts of red and yellow against a bright green backdrop. Insects buzzed their way from flower to flower, ignoring the joyful shrieks of laughter of the children running around.

The father asked the wind to lower them to the ground. The first thing he noticed was that the cheeks of the children were round and their bellies were full. Enviously he clutched his stomach, which growled loudly. Jeda noticed that the children spoke in the strange tongue of the occupier and the father's curiosity was aroused. What was this place? He noticed a young child holding a book; it was clear by the look on her face that it was speaking to her. He was thrilled. The daughters of this world were learning how to weave words.

From a distance, the father and daughter watched the happy scene. A door to a large building opened and settler women approached the children. The father was filled with fear, and he fought every urge to leap over the fence and protect the children from these monsters who had wreaked havoc on his land.

'If you touch them, I will . . .' he whispered to himself. Jeda waited to hear what action he would take, but the sentence did not end.

'He was conflicted, Jeda. He didn't know what to think. These strangers seemed gentle and kind, but he knew in his heart that they simply could not be. What he had seen and heard convinced him of that. And yet the children appeared to love them.'

They watched as the women gathered the boys and girls around them and began to tell stories – of a man who walked on water and created food for thousands from a simple woven basket. The children sighed and gasped in equal measure.

When the stories had ended, and as the women started to move everyone indoors, Jeda asked the girl, 'Did you enjoy the woman's story?' She assumed she would never hear a response, but the child must have been wondering the same thing. She turned to her father. 'Baba,' she said, 'the stories were good, but not as good as yours.'

The girl's father knelt down to embrace her, but his arms engulfed her body too easily. He could feel how small and frail she had become. He furrowed his brow as he looked at the children just a few metres away. He imagined how well they would eat that night. He thought about their soft beds, safe from the night terrors, and how he would have to snap grass stems for a makeshift bed for his daughter.

He did not sleep well the entire night afterwards.

Early the next morning, he went to fetch leaves and berries for them to eat. Jeda was pleased that she had no appetite in this world, for when he returned it was with a miserable pile of food. The girl pecked at the offering before her father raised her up.

'Don't ever forget my stories,' Jeda heard him say.

'Never, Baba!' she replied.

Jeda followed him to the walled garden. She saw him push open the gate. She saw him guide his daughter through and close the gate behind her.

'Baba?' the girl asked, confused.

'What?' cried Jeda. 'No, he can't leave her there!'

She tried to stop him, but he slowly stepped backwards. Then, spreading his arms, he called for the wind, which arrived in a gust and carried him away.

'How could you? Come back!' Jeda screamed at the girl's father.

'He had his reasons, Jeda. When the women noticed the girl alone in the garden, they welcomed her in. They stroked her hair. "Poor thing," they muttered. "Abandoned by her family."'

'It wasn't like that!' Jeda sobbed.

'"How cruel can these people be!" they said.'

'He loved her. Can't they see – he did love her!' Jeda cried.

'How could they know, Jeda? But the women took her in and loved her in their own way. So much so that they tried their hardest to rid her of her uncultured nature. They tried to teach her how to dress appropriately, how to hide her unattractive hair, how to fix her pronunciation and – importantly – they taught her to weave words. She accepted some of the teachings and rejected others, growing into a proud and brave woman, determined never to forget the stories of her father.'

'I wonder what happened to her?' Jeda mused.

'The girl grew with the other children and she thrived. In fact, she excelled so much that she became an example of how to perfectly raise these new children of the land. They trusted her, equipping her with even more knowledge. She learnt how to think like them. How to understand their delicate nature.'

'I don't understand. She became like them? Were they good or bad?' Jeda was confused.

'Wickedness is not the preserve of just one group of people. Neither is goodness. She understood this through the stories she had been raised with. The girl had also been on the receiving end of both cruelty and kindness, so, despite thinking like them, she knew she would never become them. She knew exactly who she came from. When she was grown, she found others like her. Those who understood oppression. Those who had witnessed

injustice, those filled with courage, the dreamers who could imagine a better world. She gathered them around her. They formed a powerful army and then set to work.

'They took the right words and began to pound them, knead them, pummel them into shape before unleashing them upwards. The weapons flew across the skies, high-pitched cries announced their coming, then they descended on the vicious barbed-wire fences, tearing them down and setting the captives free.'

'That's incredible!' Jeda cried. 'I wonder if her father knew what she did.'

'There was no way that he could know, save for the belief he always carried in his soul.'

'So they never met each other again?'

'They never met again. Not on Earth, at least. When the young woman saw what she had accomplished, when she felt the tingle of a new world on the horizon, she was filled with a desire to visit the place that had given and taken so much from her. She summoned a vessel and harnessed a cloud. Then she captained her way across the skies until she arrived. It was a beautiful place rich in stories, songs and music. The people marvelled at her poise and grace, how her eyes sparkled with wit and curiosity. She met a man whose eyes reminded her of the ocean and she wondered at the thinness of his lips.

'She had a daughter and she would comb her hair and tell her stories.'

Realisation dawned on Jeda and she fumbled.

'What? You mean . . . Mum? . . . You mean . . . Mum? . . . This can't . . . Mum. Mum.'

THE WORLD
OF DARKNESS

When Jeda opened her eyes, she found herself held tight in Aunty's arms. She had been delirious, talking without making sense, her eyes rolling from side to side, she was told. Jeda was embarrassed and began wiping the sides of her mouth in case of any signs of spit, unaware of having spoken anything out loud. Aunty told her how worried she had been, at first suspecting an epileptic fit or the like. She had been on the verge of calling an ambulance when she began to listen to the words pouring in waves from Jeda's lips and understood that this was not something that needed to be fixed. It was something that needed to happen. It would not be long before Jeda would discover that Aunty understood more about the box than she had let on. So Aunty waited patiently, soothing the girl's forehead and stroking her curls.

'It will soon pass,' she had whispered occasionally. 'It will soon pass.'

Then Jeda sat up abruptly and felt the urge to explain. 'I'm not crazy!'

'Of course not,' Aunty replied.

There was a long silence, as Jeda stood, went to the mirror and began to tidy herself up. For some reason she half expected the Shadowman to reappear, but only her reflection looked back. Aunty sat on the bed. Neither felt the need to speak, but questions were bubbling up inside Jeda's core. After a long time, they were released.

'Did you know about my mother?'

'What about her?'

'How she came here.'

'We all arrive in different ways.'

'Did you know of her before?'

Aunty's expression held a gentle seriousness, as though this was a conversation she had been waiting for.

'Your mother lived many lives before she passed. She did many things.'

'Did she tell you of my grandfather?'

'No.'

'She told me!' Jeda trembled slightly as she said these simple words.

There was a slight pause before Aunty asked, 'Is it what you expected?'

Jeda swallowed hard. How could she articulate the intense feelings inside her? She realised that she loved her grandfather, a man she had never met. She understood him. He gave everything. He went against expectation and duty. He had given up the most precious thing in his world and she knew why. He was amazing! Her mother, too.

'No,' she said quietly. 'It is more than I had imagined.'

'And you?'

For the first time in her life, Jeda saw her family as something truly great and she began to consider the possibility that she too might be some kind of wonderful, but inside her the Shadowman moved, quelling the thought. It was at that moment Jeda realised that not once had she heard his voice inside her in the world of story. He could not get to her. He was powerless there and she knew that was why he wanted the box. He needed to maintain control. Jeda immediately challenged herself to focus on something to quieten his voice. She looked around and saw the wooden box on the floor. The lid had been shut.

'I closed it!' Aunty said, noticing the observation. 'I thought it was better that way. You have been through a lot. These stories have power and you should rest for now.'

'Aunty, I need to go back!'

'Daughter, you need to rest.'

'But there is more in there. I need to know!'

'Jeda, you don't understand. These stories have power. You need to be stronger to survive them.'

'Aunty, I am safe in there.'

Jeda tried to pick the box off the floor but inside her the Shadowman furiously tried to compel her to place it back down. Her fingers found the latch. He fought back, but she strained to lift it and, by sheer force, as it came free, the stories began to swirl in a dizzying display. Aunty cowered in a corner, avoiding being hit by the gold and silver sparkles. A golden firefly hit the tip of Jeda's finger, sending a shockwave through her body, making her fall backwards.

Aunty jumped up to catch her. 'Daughter, daughter. What have you done?'

• • •

Jeda found herself floating in a brilliant blue sky surrounded by clouds, some large, soft and white, others more threatening, their dark grey edges towering above her. She could bounce along on a cloud, pieces of which seemed to break off, forming a series of pillowy steps that led down to a grassy plain through which meandered a red dirt road. She stepped off the clouds onto the road, instinctively turning to the right, and began to follow the narrow, winding path. In the distance she could make out a village.

As she headed towards it, around her a familiar voice returned.

'There was once a chief, who had a beautiful daughter. Her name was Sanida. Everyone who encountered her saw a form of beauty. Some say it was the way she dressed, with bracelets that joyfully announced her arrival. Others say it was the humour with which she responded to questions, and yet others said it was the care she gave to the people around her. But most people recognised that she had a very special gift. She was a giver of joy. When she saw someone in despair, she would gift them a story and soothe their souls. If she saw someone in pain, she would gift them a story that would raise their spirits. She allowed people to imagine an alternative life, far removed from their difficult situation. She made them laugh and cry and dream. They loved her.'

At that moment, Jeda heard the sounds of bracelets jingling. She looked up and saw a mother and child seated under a tree. Sanida walked towards them, then knelt before the mother and gently caressed the child's cheek with her fingers, receiving a shy smile in return.

'Hello, little one. I heard you cry last night. Shall I tell you a story?' Jeda saw Sanida's hands and lips move in unison, weaving a series of words that captivated her small audience. The encounter was brief, but at the end the child reached out her tiny hand and touched the woman's face as a token of thanks. Then Sanida stood, her entourage close behind, and continued on her way. Jeda followed them home.

As Jeda was aware that her presence went unnoticed, she walked behind Sanida directly into her house and looked around. The earthen walls kept it cool, and high above her head an intricate thatch roof allowed a gentle breeze to circulate. Jeda was delighted by the colourful fabrics and ran her fingers over the solid, carved wooden furniture. It was soon evening, and when Sanida finally lay down on her bed and closed her eyes, Jeda watched her chest rise and fall, her expression changing with her dreams.

Her mother's words again began to fill her head.

'Jeda, there is an invisible line that divides the human world from the World of Darkness, and while Sanida had many admirers who sought her affections, she did not know that a Shadow from the other world was watching too. The more he watched her, the more he desired her. He could not stop thinking about her. He wanted to own and possess her. But he knew he could not simply cross over into the human world without a physical form. He needed a plan. So he decided that he would first pass through the land of the recently deceased.

'This he did, and as he wandered about he came across a skilled carpenter, with fine, elegant fingers, whose untimely death had been brought about by an unpleasant encounter between a blade and his chest. He saw the fingernails glisten. He saw the delicate gesticulations and asked if he might borrow those hands for just a short period of time. The carpenter agreed. He removed his hands and handed them to the Shadow, who took them and placed them onto his form.'

Jeda wondered if Sanida suspected the Shadow was near, as she suddenly trembled and turned in her sleep. She could picture the Shadow visiting those new souls coming to terms with their early demise and begging them for their body parts. As though Rahami could read her thoughts, the voice continued.

'Yes. He pleaded for their thick heads of hair, their rippling stomachs, their firm thighs that curved and gleamed. He demanded a rich voice that spoke several tongues, thick lips, taut buttocks. He took them all and attached them to his form. Then, adorning himself with clothes stitched together with gold and silver thread, he stepped across the invisible line into the world of the humans.'

The following morning, there was a sound of great excitement. The village women were ululating loudly, waving banners of pink and yellow flowers, while the envious eyes of the men looked on disapprovingly, as a handsome young stranger approached the village.

The people were so drawn to his exceptional beauty that they forgot themselves.

He walked like a God.

He danced like a Demon.

He showered them with gifts and praise.

They welcomed him warmly, washing his feet, as was their custom, and serving him whatever was needed to quench his thirst and satiate his hunger. He was polite, extending his gratitude, but his eyes hungrily sought out his prize.

Jeda knew immediately who this stranger was. When she saw Sanida approach him, she tried to issue a warning, for Sanida too was dazzled by his beauty and power.

However, it is not easy to hide your true self for long periods of time, and Jeda saw him itch and scratch. She saw him snap and grimace, jerking his head to one side as he rolled his tongue around his teeth, trying to familiarise himself with this new physical form. Sanida was a giver of joy, a people watcher, and she began to notice that something was amiss with the stranger and so she slowly started to distance herself from him. Jeda breathed a sigh of relief and was filled with a great sense of satisfaction, as Sanida returned to her home and busied herself threading beads.

'I wish I could tell you, my darling, that Sanida continued living the life she had always lived. But do you think the Shadow was going to let her go so easily? Not at all. His intention was to take her home, and he would not leave without fulfilling that goal. He waited until the dead of night to put his plan into action.'

Jeda was lying on a mat when she saw him enter Sanida's home. He grabbed the sleeping girl and attempted to carry her off, but she woke with a start and instinctively began to kick and scream. Jeda leapt onto him, trying to pull him off.

'Let her go! Let her go!' Jeda cried, fists flailing.

But the Shadow felt not a thing.

Jeda raced after him, as he marched towards the invisible line.

'Bite him. Scratch him!' she commanded and, as though she heard, Sanida did so with abandon. She hit and kicked and clawed and screamed, but he was too strong. He was too powerful. He carried Sanida far from her world and crossed back into the world of shadows.

•   •   •

Jeda was filled with dread, but she followed, and as soon as they had crossed the line they were plunged into darkness. The air was filled with the musty smell of decay. Jeda listened for the repetitive thud of the Shadow's footsteps as he marched towards his home. Gradually, as her eyes became accustomed to the gloom, Jeda could make out the shapes of shadowy figures shifting about.

The Shadow placed Sanida on the ground and shoved her forward, growling that she must now walk. She trembled, but her senses told her that no matter how loudly she screamed in this place, nobody would hear.

'Where am I?' she asked. The Shadow did not reply. Instead, they marched on to the land of the recently deceased, where he began to return the borrowed body parts, piece after piece, until all that was left was a obscure, pulsing, grey figure.

When they finally arrived at his home, the Shadow pointed to the door and Sanida dutifully stepped inside. A foul odour filled her nostrils; the floor was littered with the bones of rats and other small animals. The cobwebs were so numerous they stuck to her hair, her clothes and her skin. She shuddered and rubbed them off with such ferocity she bruised her skin. Sanida huddled in a corner, wishing that the world would swallow her up and she would disappear forever.

Jeda was desperate to tell her she was not alone, so despite knowing she could not be heard, she quietly sang the songs her mother had sung to her when she was a child and whispered words of comfort.

'Sanida, you don't know me, but you are not alone!' She placed her invisible arms around Sanida's terrified body and held her tight.

After some time, Jeda saw Sanida wipe her tears and emerge from the little round house to look around. They were both astonished at what she saw. There were hundreds of houses, very similar to the one they found themselves in now, and they were not alone, for occupying them were others like Sanida who had been taken against their will.

It took some time before the occupants realised that Sanida was a giver of joy, and they immediately planned to meet in secret, where Sanida found strength by whispering her stories, soothing souls and reassuring the suffering.

'*Sanida gave hope to all those around her and they gave her the only thing they could,*' Rahami said.

'What could they possibly give her in a place like this?' Jeda wondered, looking around at the grey dust and rising ash.

'*They taught her how to survive. She survived by doing exactly what she was told to do, whenever she was told to do it. She survived by remaining silent when he disrobed her, for he could do whatever he wanted because he owned her. She gave birth to the Shadow's children. Sons and daughters that she did not want, but when she held them in her arms she could not help but love them.*'

Jeda watched as Sanida cried out in pain, held down by those who came to help, as she delivered her fourth child. The sweat poured from her face, her neck and her chest. She panted heavily, then strained as the birthing pains arrived in full force.

'Please be okay,' Jeda breathed.

The child arrived screeching furiously, and Sanida's companions wrapped him up to keep him warm then handed him to his mother. She hesitated at first, then reached out her arms and took him. She stared down at the little boy, his lower lip sticking out as though he had been terribly wronged, and immediately she fell in love. His black eyes gazed up at her and he appeared transfixed by the vision of beauty above him. But his hunger soon took priority, so he opened his mouth and let loose his demands. She acquiesced and soon he was suckling happily.

The weeks turned into months, which turned into years, but for Jeda time was irrelevant. She stayed and watched Sanida go about her daily business. She scrubbed and cooked and cleaned and washed and polished, doing everything that was asked of her.

'Fetch!' the Shadow roared, and Sanida would race away.

'Come!' he bellowed, and Sanida would leave whatever she was doing and await instruction.

'Go!' he commanded, and if she moved too slowly he would seize a nearby stick and strike her with it.

Jeda was painfully aware that the joy on Sanida's face was far diminished. She realised it had been a long time since she had seen Sanida smile.

One morning, as Sanida lay asleep on her mat, the Shadow stood solemnly over her. Scowling, he kicked her in the ribs and screamed, 'Go and fetch some water, you lazy creature!'

Jeda felt Sanida's pain and exhaustion. 'I wish you didn't have to go,' she whispered to herself.

Her mother's voice swirled around.

'Ah, but water was needed. Sanida decided to leave the children at home. She picked up a clay pot and followed the winding path through the World of Darkness, stumbling over stones and the roots of dead trees on her way to collect water from the river. She always went to the same spot, believing

that this was the cleanest and purest water that she would be able to find,
but never quite certain of its quality, as it was always clouded in grey.

'On this particular day, as Sanida approached the water hole and
prepared to lean in and fill her pots, the water began to swirl and churn.
Then, without warning, from out of the depths rose an old woman, a frightening creature whose back and shoulders were hunched. Her shrivelled
breasts drooped to the ground. Her tiny frame was held together by ashen
skin and the hair on her head grew in thin, grey clumps.'

At a slight distance from the water hole, Jeda saw Sanida collapse
to the ground, quivering with fear. Jeda recoiled when she noticed
the old woman, who seemed to hover above the water. Neither she
nor Sanida had encountered this grotesque being before, and as the
old woman opened her mouth to speak they saw her rotting gums,
to which clung two blackened teeth. Strands of sticky saliva lined her
foul-smelling mouth and her eyes were covered with a grey film that
appeared to stare beyond Sanida into the nothing. She raised a finger
and pointed in Sanida's direction.

'You do not belong here. If you stay, you will die here, like me,'
the old woman gasped, as though finding the energy to speak. 'Cross
the line. You do not belong here.' Her voice creaked with the ravages
of time, sending a shudder down Jeda's spine.

Though horrified, Sanida leaned forward slowly, for as she looked
more closely at the old woman she was filled with an overwhelming
sense of familiarity. Sanida reached out her fingers to touch the
woman's hand, but as suddenly as she had appeared the old woman
sunk back down into the depths.

Utterly shaken, Sanida stood, then she raced home, closely
followed by Jeda. The unfilled pots remained by the water hole.

They entered the house and Sanida slammed the door behind her, panting heavily. The words of the old woman swirled around her head. They bothered her.

Just then, the four children entered the room and immediately headed towards their mother, fingers outstretched, faces beaming. Sanida embraced them. As she did so, she looked into their eyes and realised the old woman was right. She did not belong here and neither did her children. They were too full of curiosity, too full of life. She knew that she had to do something, and quickly, before she changed her mind.

The Shadow had left the house and he would not return for some time, so Sanida strapped her two youngest children to her body. She slowly opened the door and peered around. There was nobody in sight, so seizing the hands of the older children, she slipped out and started to run. Jeda followed, her heart pounding in her chest. They ran so hard that the grey ashy dust flew up around them.

As Jeda ran, Rahami continued the story.

'"Run! Run, child! The line is not too far away." Sanida believed that if she could just make it to the invisible line – if she could just cross over – then she would be able to return home. A beautiful wish, indeed. But far across the World of Darkness the Shadow was perplexed. Something did not feel right and he decided to return to his home. He immediately saw that the door was open and the house was quiet, no longer filled with the hushed voices to which he was accustomed. He saw Sanida's footprints in the dust and followed them at great speed. It did not take long for him to spot her. She was struggling to keep pace, held back by the weight of two children on her back and two others by her side.

'He tore after her with a high-pitched shriek. Sanida turned to see him heading straight for her. She gasped and tried to pick up speed, but her children were still so small. They did not understand and started to cry.

'"Keep moving, children," she begged. "It is not much further."

'But one of her sons, although he tried, could not move his legs fast enough. He stumbled and fell, and hearing the rush of the Shadow behind her Sanida wailed as she tried to drag him along the ground, unable to leave him. But it was no use. The Shadow was too fast. He caught her and dragged her back to the house, then slammed her to the ground. He left the room, only to return moments later with a spinning wheel, which he flung at her, then commanded her to spin her hair into gold. Sanida was filled with rage and refused, so he punched and kicked her. Then, grabbing a rod, he raised it high above his head and brought it down. Sanida screamed with pain.'

Jeda watched with horror as the Shadow stood bent over this woman whom she now knew so well, yelling and screeching with abandon. Sanida saw her four children huddled in a corner, whimpering, tears and snot smeared across their faces.

'Turn around!' she ordered breathlessly. Her children did as she asked. Sanida then wailed as the Shadow beat her till her blood flowed into the ground.

Jeda cried with her until she could not stand by any longer. Though she knew she had no power or influence in this world, every part of her wanted to attack. She seized objects and flung them at the Shadow, yelling every obscenity, then lunged at him, pulling and tearing. For a moment, the Shadow paused, as though suddenly aware of her presence, but then he resumed the beating. Only when Sanida was too exhausted to fight back did he appear satisfied. He stood, breathing hard, then lowered the stick and casually cast it to one side.

'You will spin your hair into gold,' he commanded.

And with that he left.

Jeda was not sure if Sanida was so broken that somehow her spirit sensed that someone else was there, but after a long time, as Sanida struggled to her feet, Jeda was convinced that she clutched at her knee for support.

Jeda watched as Sanida took in the room through her bloody eye and saw her children fearfully watching her. She looked at the spinning wheel and the chair in front of it, silently waiting. She swallowed hard. She had no choice.

'She plucked a hair from her head and placed it in the wheel, Jeda. And then took another and another. The wheel began to turn and, as it did, she saw the shiny blackness slowly turn brown, then red, then orange and yellow, until it was a fiery gold, shimmering and filling the room with light. She spun until her fingers were raw. She spun until the gold piled high around her. She spun until her hair grew in thin grey clumps and her shoulders began to stoop.'

Jeda saw the Shadow crow with delight, as time and time again he helped himself to the gold. Jeda watched as the months passed and Sanida became thinner. She saw her skin become ashen, but she was not alone. Sanida's four children watched with anguish as their mother withered away. They saw her joy fading and tried desperately to remind her of who she was.

'Tell us a story, Mama.'

For the first time in a long time, Jeda saw the edges of Sanida's mouth turn upwards in a faint smile. She looked at her children and remembered that she was their mother. So, as she spun her gold she spun stories. She told them of the tiny spirits who visited babies while they slept and made them giggle and laugh. She told them of mighty warriors who, with no thought of peril, fought for freedom and justice. Jeda watched as Sanida waved an imaginary sword in the air, telling the children, 'She took a sword and rode across the plains. She raised her sword to the sky and she charged and she slashed and she slayed.'

'Jeda,' her mother's voice exclaimed, '*it was at that moment that Sanida saw the joy in those tiny faces and remembered the words of the old woman. She did not belong here. They did not belong here. She knew that she had to leave. She spun until the Shadow demanded to eat, then she cooked and fed him a rich meal. When he had eaten his fill, he flung his dish at her and went to lie down. She waited until the sound of deep sleep filled the air, then, clutching the hands of her children, she slipped out of the house and she ran.*'

Once more Jeda found herself racing through the World of Darkness. In front of her, Sanida ran, pulling her four children behind her. The ground was rough. Dust and ash filled their nostrils but still they ran. They tripped over roots in the ground, over rocks and stones they could barely make out in the dim light. Sanida dared not look at the houses around them for fear it may slow her down, but Jeda noticed the curious faces peering out, wondering what was going on. Some knew and wished they had the courage to do the same. For hours they ran, until in the distance they noticed the air looked different. It was somehow less dull and weighty. Jeda was convinced that there lay the invisible line.

'Run, Sanida! Run!' Jeda shouted.

Sanida drew on every last ounce of strength she possessed and the pace increased. 'Almost there. We're almost there!' she encouraged her children.

Determined to please their mother, the children pressed on. Their feet hurt, but they did not complain. They were desperate for water, but they did not stop to ask. Faster and faster they ran, spurred on by Sanida's encouraging words.

'But while they ran towards freedom, Jeda,' Rahami continued, *'the Shadow awakened from his sleep. He noticed the warmth had gone from his house and he shouted for Sanida to light a fire. He was filled with rage when there was no response and so, angrily, he raised himself from his bed and picked up a stick. When he saw that Sanida was not there, he needed to unleash his anger and headed to where the children slept, but he was horrified to find the mats lay bare. He saw the door was open and marched outside. He closed his eyes and, peering into the darkness, he could see that*

far away Sanida was approaching the invisible line, their four children in tow, and there was . . . something else too, something different.

'He raged, smashing the walls of his house. The audacity! After everything that he had done for her. He immediately set out after her, enlisting help from other Shadows. They formed a seething mass, merging and melting into each other. They moved quickly, calling for more assistance as they went, until soon there were hundreds of them tearing after the one who dared to resist.'

Jeda wished she could scoop up the children who, now exhausted, lagged behind their desperate mother.

'Move, move!' she urged. The children wailed and did as they were asked, fearful of the inevitable whipping they would receive as they heard the terrifying rush of movement, the hideous wails and screeches of a thousand Shadows and Demons behind them. But there before her was a thin sliver of light. She was so close, so close. The Shadows were fast approaching, tumbling over themselves to get to her, clawing and reaching, seeking to drag her down. The line was within reach, just a few more steps.

But just as she was about to cross they caught her. They fell on her. They pinned her arms behind her back. They crushed her neck with their knees.

Jeda scrambled over them, trying to reach Sanida as she gasped.

'I can't breathe, I can't breathe, I can't breathe.'

But they refused to hear Sanida. They refused to see her eyes close. They refused to see her body soften.

'Please!' Jeda begged. Her voice went unheard, save for the ears of one Shadow, whose eyes narrowed as he peered around. He slowly moved in Jeda's direction.

As she lay on the ground, Sanida felt her light slowly begin to fade, then she heard the tiny, breaking voice of a child.

'Mama, Mama. Remember, she took her sword and she raced across the plains. She raised it to the sky and she charged and she slashed and she slayed. Mama, Mama.'

Jeda watched as Sanida slowly opened her eyes and saw her children, their little faces filled with hope and love. In that instant, she knew that they were givers of joy and their joy gave her strength. She rose up, flinging the Shadows off her. They flew at her but her presence was too powerful. She swatted them off like pesky flies. The Shadows screamed, but their sounds were barely audible to Sanida, who took her children by the hand and marched towards the line. She paused, closed her eyes, inhaled deeply, then she crossed.

AUNTY THE HEALER

'Oh Jeda, it would have been wonderful if she had gone home, found her family and lived happily ever after, but you shall soon see that this is not that kind of tale,' Rahami's voice warned gently.

As Jeda made her way to the invisible line, she was deeply moved to see the children wrap themselves around their mother. Her heart was filled with joy as she watched them stride towards their old world, oblivious to the Shadows who tried in vain to reach across the line. Jeda was unaware of the Shadow that had detected her unusual presence and, although he could not see her, he sensed her energy was ripe and it drove him mad. He raced around like a hunter, trying to locate the source. He sniffed hard until at last he found it and just as Jeda crossed the line after Sanida and her family he raised his hand, stretched out his twisted fingers, then sliced at the air with his claws. To anyone present, it may have looked like nothing at all, but Jeda immediately felt a searing pain in her arm. A large gash appeared on her skin and the filthy ash from the World of Darkness rushed into her veins, clouding her eyes and causing her to collapse to the ground.

The pain was unbearable and Jeda screamed loudly as her body struggled to fight the vile substance. She tried to pull herself further from the invisible line, a desperate attempt to distance herself from the pain, but it seemed to intensify the further she moved away.

'Sanida! Sanida, help me!' she begged, extending her arm, but Sanida could not hear. Jeda wailed uncontrollably as Sanida slowly walked away, looking around her old world as though seeing it for the very first time.

Jeda was doubled up in agony, groaning and trying to control the pain when she suddenly felt a sharp slap on her cheek. Again and again came the hard, sharp pain, making Jeda wince.

'No, please, no!' she wailed.

She detected the faint odour of warm bread and cinnamon, and could make out a loud, anxious voice. 'Jeda, daughter! Come back! Come back!'

The familiarity of Aunty amidst this intense misery was almost too much for Jeda to bear. She began to weep uncontrollably and saw that she was on her knees, clinging desperately to Aunty's skirts. Aunty took some yellow grass, wove it into a crude tourniquet and bound it round her arm. A nearby tree bore yellow fruits. Aunty stood and plucked several of them. She sliced into the soft, juicy flesh of one of them and hollowed out a container. She then squeezed the juice from the other fruits into the empty shell. Taking a razor blade from a pouch, she began to cut tiny incisions around the gash.

Jeda was in so much pain she barely noticed what was happening. Aunty then poured the juice into the incisions, which began to bubble and foment violently. The white froth turned grey, then black, until with a vicious hiss the ash exploded through the gash,

screeching as it crossed back into the World of Darkness.

Jeda sobbed as Aunty delicately stitched the skin back together. When it was over, they sat under the tree, waiting for the pain to lessen.

'How . . .' Jeda began.

'Is it important?' Aunty replied. She struggled to her feet and then reached out a hand. Jeda grabbed it and pulled herself up. For

several moments, they walked on in silence, a million questions swirling around Jeda's mind. The weaver birds building their nests in the nearby trees around them chattered incessantly, filling the air with magic.

'How did you find me?' Jeda finally asked.

'I was there when you opened the box. I held you as your eyes closed. I wiped the sweat when you needed, and when I knew you were in pain I had no choice but to follow you.'

'You didn't come sooner.'

'I didn't need to. I have lived my own stories and my grandmother gifted me many of hers before she passed.'

Jeda looked at the tourniquet around her arm.

'Did she also teach you how to cure people?'

Aunty smiled and walked on for a moment before replying.

'She taught me many things.'

There was another silence.

'But, Aunty, I thought you believed all those things were bad.'

'Why would you say that?'

'Because when you took me to church that day, that's what they said.'

'Daughter, I believe in God and I pray every single day. But I come from a great line of healers. Why would I throw that knowledge away?'

Jeda wondered about this. She knew her mother had friends who condemned as evil or wicked those who practised the old knowledge. She had watched them with fascination and hope as they'd placed hands on her mother, closed their eyes and let passages from holy books pour from their throats, banishing the evil spirits causing harm on her, and raising an army of invisible warriors to watch over her.

She had once heard one of them whisper quietly that until Rahami believed, she would never be healed. When Jeda had asked her mother about this, she was told that people believe in lots of different things and it was okay.

'Aunty, you believe in stories?'

'They show us who we are and so you must be careful of the ones you listen to. I know many people who think they know every-thing, yet when I point towards the moon all they see is my finger. Their worlds are very small. But you – your mother has given you a great gift. Treasure it! Not everyone has this chance.'

At that moment, they saw a small village in the distance and a group of travellers heading purposefully towards it. The village looked vaguely familiar and Jeda recognised it as Sanida's old home.

'Aunty, come with me. The story is not finished.'

•　　　•　　　•

Rahami's rich words soon filled the air.

'*Sanida was filled with great excitement as she made her way through her old world. She told her children about her childhood, how she had swum in the river and scrambled from trees. She spoke to them of her grandmother, and how pleased she would be to see them. She warned them that her father, despite being stern, would do anything for his family and was full of love and kindness, and he had a fondness for the fruit of the mabuyu tree. The children were filled with wonder and expectation and could not wait to try this special fruit. The light and colour and the sound of birds chirruping filled them with such happiness they did not mind the long, hot march.*'

Jeda and Aunty finally caught up with them, in time to listen to their excited chatter of what might lie ahead.

'We will eat the freshest fruit. Watermelon juice will drip down your chins. They may slaughter a cow for us and welcome us home. We will eat cassava and yam until our bellies ache.'

Sanida began to reel off a list of foods: coconut, steamed beans, maize, fish with special spices, doughballs with cinnamon, tiny, crispy deep-fried titbits. Aunty began to cluck with joy, beaming at the thought, then exclaimed loudly, 'Yes! Take me there now!'

'Aunty, they can't hear you!' Jeda told her.

'I know. Don't kill my dream!' came the playful retort.

As Sanida approached the village, Jeda noticed a change in her demeanour. While she continued to smile brightly, it seemed as though her excitement was now tinged with some trepidation. She walked more slowly and her voice quietened as she looked from house to house. The village was still, with nobody around.

Her world had changed. Jeda watched a bewildered expression grow on her face.

'Hello, is anyone there?' Sanida called out.

There was no response.

'Can anyone hear me?'

Only the sound of birds and insects came in reply.

'Can anybody see me?' she questioned quietly, half to herself.

An old man emerged from his little house and peered at Sanida through eyes that had not seen clearly for many years. The grey film that covered them forced him to step closer towards her for a better look. Sanida could not recall ever having seen him before.

'Grandfather, do you know me?' she asked politely.

The old man placed his hands on her face and her hair. His fingers searched the heads and faces of the children, trying to recognise their features, but they were strangers to him. He shook his head and slowly shuffled back towards his home.

Sanida saw him push against a door that was hanging off its hinges. She looked up to the roof and saw the holes in the thatch. She observed that every house around her seemed uncared for and shabby, a far cry from the beautiful homesteads in which she had grown. The flowering bushes that had once attracted insects and butterflies had been hacked down. Many of the magnificent trees that formed a forested backdrop to their village were no longer in existence. She stood silent for a long time, struggling to take it in.

Jeda felt the same way. She remembered the beauty and vitality of the village, yet now it seemed worn, as though it were slowly dying.

'This village is dead!' Aunty exclaimed matter-of-factly.

'It wasn't like this before. Something happened,' Jeda replied.

At that moment a trickle of bodies slowly wandered back into the village. They dragged themselves forward as though each step was an effort. Sanida ran towards them, asking them if they knew her father or her grandfather. She seized their hands, searching their eyes for recognition, but met with none. They retreated from her, as though she were a mad woman whose eyes blazed with a desperate fire.

Rahami's voice trembled, as her words filled the air. *'She struggled to find somebody that she knew, but to no avail. In that moment Sanida realised that she had been away for such a long time that nobody recognised her any more. Nobody recognised her children. She, in turn, did not know who they were. With horror, she saw that she belonged nowhere. In desperation, she turned and ran through the village, screaming into the houses, calling herself into existence.'*

Jeda and Aunty watched as Sanida banged on doors, yelled through windows, pushed her way into people's homes before being violently thrown out.

'I am Sanida, daughter of Chief Bohero, granddaughter of Chief Mekati, great warrior and queen,' she cried. 'My mother was Aziza the Wise. Please. Somebody must know me,' she sobbed. 'Somebody must know me!' She fell to the ground, broken-hearted, wailing gently, her tears staining the sandy soil beneath.

Jeda and Aunty watched, unable to comfort her and trying not to weep. They watched as slowly she gathered her children close to her and wiped away her tears, leaving great smears on her cheeks in the process. They watched as she exhaled deeply, pushed her chest out, then led her children back towards the line.

'Is she going back?' asked Jeda.

'It is not over for her,' replied Aunty.

Rahami's voice continued. *'It was certainly not over for Sanida. She gathered her strength, then marched, determined, towards the world that had held her hostage, and she peered in. Across the invisible line she could make out the forms of thousands of people trapped in the World of Darkness. This place had robbed her of everything. She had nothing. She was nothing.*

'She felt an anger burn in the pit of her stomach. It rose higher, filling her chest, entering her throat. She flung her arms wide and she raged. Her anger, her strength, her light smashed down the barrier between the human world and the world of the shadows, and it was then that she saw with new eyes what she had helped to create.

'Magnificent buildings stretched tall, crafted from the gold she had spun and the blood that she had shed. The finest things were enjoyed by the Shadows, while around them those like her remained in the corners. This was a world that she had not been privy to and yet now her eyes were opened it was all clear.

'She realised that she belonged in this world as well as the world from which she had come. She had suffered too much to let it go. She had bled too much. She had given too much and now her children would reap the benefits. She marched between the worlds with her children, staking her claim. She did not realise that now the line that separated the worlds no longer existed, the Shadows were free to move like ghosts between worlds.'

Jeda and Aunty watched as Sanida made her way across the worlds, with a strength and confidence that Jeda had not seen before.

She was coming to terms with her new life.

Jeda was slightly envious. She too had sometimes felt lost, but was it this simple? To simply believe that you belong? Surely it had to be more than that. She saw Sanida continue to be her true self, a giver of joy. It made Jeda wonder what her purpose was. When Sanida saw someone who was in pain, she would gift them a story and heal them. If she saw someone who was feeling low, she would gift them a story and raise their spirits. If anybody challenged her, she spoke out, but she felt free to be whoever she was, and if anyone challenged her she would quickly put them in their place.

• • •

'She came too late!' Jeda and Aunty looked up, alarmed at the voice, and caught sight of an old woman approaching. She was hobbling and, with great effort, sat down on a broken log next to them.

'Grandmother, what do you know of this place?' Jeda asked, indicating towards the broken houses and lost souls.

'I know stories,' she croaked.

'Why did you not tell Sanida? She wanted to know!'

'The time was not right. She is beginning a new journey and the stories I have would have filled her with unimaginable grief. First, let her find strength. She will return.'

'Grandmother, you can tell me.'

'I heard that Aziza the Wise was broken-hearted at the loss of her daughter and never truly recovered.' Jeda thought for a while, trying to make sense of these words. She had never once considered how much suffering those left behind would have endured.

'What of her father and her grandmother?'

'That is perhaps a story that you do not wish to hear,' the old voice replied.

•   •   •

Jeda's skin began to tingle and she felt something hover around her. Its breath was hot; as it lay thick on the curve of her neck, she heard a low, deep snarl in her ear. The wound that Aunty had stitched together began to itch and like an animal driven mad by fleas Jeda began to scratch.

'What is the matter with you?' Aunty asked, but Jeda could not answer. She clawed at her skin incessantly until suddenly her wound burst open and black blood poured out. Another gash appeared on her, then another, and another. The Shadow had found her and it attacked with such ferocity that she howled.

Aunty howled with her, then she grabbed a nearby branch studded with thorns and waved it around them, screeching and praying as loudly as she could. With one almighty scream, Aunty succeeded in pulling them out of the world and they fell backwards, gasping for breath, onto Jeda's bedroom floor.

Jeda was in a daze. She crawled around the carpet as though feeling for a lost object, a strange drone-like wail emitting from her lips.

Aunty grabbed her and held on to her.

'Rest, child. Rest.'

Jeda's eyes closed.

•   •   •

When Jeda awoke, she was lying in bed. Aunty was fussing and mopping the swollen beads of sweat that rolled down her face with a damp towel. Aunty reached across and lifted a glass of water to Jeda's lips.

'Drink.'

It was gentle but authoritative, and Jeda allowed the cool liquid to slowly swirl around her mouth. She lay her head back on the pillow, contemplating everything that had taken place. She soon began to feel more alive.

'I really want to know that story.'

Aunty refused to respond, continuing to fuss silently, her face holding a stony expression.

'Aunty,' Jeda repeated. 'I said I want to know.'

'I heard what you said,' came the reply. 'Look at yourself. What do you see?'

Jeda looked down and saw that her entire body was a patchwork of bandages and gauzes.

'Do you have any idea what happened in there?'

Jeda recalled the incessant and deeply uncomfortable feeling of somebody watching her. She remembered the agonising pain, as something wicked sliced into her. She remembered believing that she was just not strong enough to bear it until somehow Aunty freed them from that place. But the old woman . . . what she had said . . . Jeda needed to know.

'Daughter' – Aunty looked her in the eye – 'I promised your mother that I would keep you safe. Allow me to keep that promise.'

Jeda loved Aunty. She wanted to make her happy. Yet something called to her and, having listened to the stories her mother had wanted her to hear, it was clear that she needed to do what she felt was right, even if it meant disappointing people along the way. She held Aunty's hand and spoke to her in a language she thought she would understand.

'Aunty, you have already kept your promise and you will continue to keep it when I return, but you once told me that when you hear the drum beating you must dance to its rhythm. You need to let me go.'

Aunty chuckled. 'When did you get so wise?'

Jeda embraced Aunty, as she gave her silent blessing. The hug was so warm and soft and homely that Jeda did not want to be released, but finally Aunty stroked her hair and insisted on cooking her something to keep her strength up. They ate, and when the meal was finished Jeda climbed the stairs to her bedroom and picked up the box. Inside her, the Shadowman stirred, desperate to try again.

'You don't have to disappoint Aunty,' he insisted. 'She has done so much for you. She will be happier if you stayed.'

Jeda held the box till Aunty called out, 'I will be here until your father arrives. If you need me, just call. Do what you need to do.'

Jeda's fingers touched the latch and lifted it. She raised the lid and the stories poured out. Jeda reached up and, as her feet lifted off the ground, she focused on the old woman.

'Please send me there. Please send me there.'

THE OLD WOMAN TELLS HER STORY

Jeda plunged into a new world, rolling onto soft, yellow grass, but the old woman was nowhere to be found. For hours, Jeda wandered around in desperation, calling loudly, 'Hello, is anyone there?'

Her feet began to ache and she wondered whether Aunty was right. Perhaps this was a mistake. Perhaps she had heard all that she needed to hear. She did not know the way home, so she decided to sit and rest under the branches of a nearby tree. It was then that she realised she was parched, but when she looked around there was no sign of any rivers or any lakes. There was nothing.

'I am thirsty,' she yelled, but there was no response.

'Mama!' Still nothing.

'I want some water,' she announced angrily, and before her eyes a calabash sprouted from the tree branch above her and began to grow. It grew bigger and bigger, and when it finally stopped growing Jeda reached up and plucked it from the branch. It was so heavy that she almost dropped it, but when she peered inside she saw that it was full of cool, crystal-clear water. She drank greedily and once her thirst had been quenched, she looked back up at the tree branch and understood that the calabash had only begun to grow when she had asked for it.

Then she realised. This was not a story her mother had chosen for her; this was a story she had chosen for herself and she had the power to take it anywhere she wanted. With her back to the tree, she cried out, 'Grandmother, I wish to hear your story.'

There was a rustling behind a nearby bush and, as Jeda waited in fascination, she saw the old, hunched woman once more hobbling towards her.

'You have come for a story. Let me rest my legs and then I will begin.'

Jeda immediately dragged a great log towards the old woman and helped her sit down.

•   •   •

The wrinkled grandmother held on to her stick as she made herself comfortable, stretching out one leg, then the other, before leaning forward. She ran her grey tongue over her wrinkled lips, moistening them, then she began to speak.

'There was once a broken chief. He was broken because he had lost his only daughter and, no matter where he sought her, she was nowhere to be found. He tried to console himself by focusing on the achievements of his other children, but the loss was great and his enormous guilt of all the things he could have done to keep her safe stayed with him every day.'

Jeda knew instinctively that this was Sanida's father. She felt sorry for him, as he would never know what happened to his daughter.

She wondered if the old woman knew, but before she had a chance to ask, the old woman continued.

'Chief Bohero had a powerful sense of duty and tried to keep the spirit of the village alive. Indeed, it thrived, with each individual understanding their responsibility towards others. He ensured that fairness and kindness were at the heart of every transaction.

'Now, you should know that the chief was a formidable hunter. Whenever he left the village to hunt, he was confident that every arrow he fired would hit its mark and every snare would trap his intended prey. This had earned him great respect.

'One day, as the chief sat with the elders in council, they received word that strangers were due to arrive in the village. A party was sent out to greet them and welcome them into their midst.'

Jeda remembered how her mother would always cook extra food, just in case somebody happened to come by unannounced, and if the strangers were many she would find a way to make the food go round. She remembered how this had sometimes annoyed her father, who would have preferred that they wait and finish their meal once the visitors had left. The memory pleased her.

'The chief knew that the level of hospitality to any stranger who approached was a reflection on the entire community and so preparations were made. Strangers were considered a blessing who offered insight into the world beyond, so when they arrived, they were fed, watered and given rest. There was nothing that was too much trouble.'

Jeda understood this well. She had always instinctively made a drink for a guest. She had once innocently asked Aunty if she would like a drink. The harsh retort was swift: 'If I beg for water, will it quench my thirst?'

Ever since, Jeda had provided refreshment as a matter of course.

'The guests arrived and were pleased with the attention shown to them. They offered small trinkets as gifts, which pleased the community greatly; however, when after two days the strangers showed little intention of moving on, the chief began to ask questions. Where had they been and what had been their reception? As messengers returned with worrying news of what they had discovered, the chief learnt too late that wherever the visitors had travelled, they had been filled with a desire to stay.

'It was then that he saw how their eyes glazed when they looked upon the enormous, glistening fruits that hung from the branches. He saw how hungrily their eyes devoured the wonder of the magnificent trees surrounding them. How they swallowed hard when the beautiful women walked past, and how they questioned the young men excitedly when they learnt of strange and magnificent stones that glittered in the nearby hills.'

Jeda wondered how Sanida's father might ask them to leave, as she imagined it would be an unforgivable act.

'The chief and the elders consulted the Oracle and asked what they should do. The Oracle cast down the stones, studied them, listened to them, then issued a stark warning that a great serpent, born of the strangers, would eventually spew fire and ash across their land. The chief was perplexed and decided to visit their neighbouring village to see the truth with his own eyes.

'The chief was horrified to find it unrecognisable. The filth poured down the streets. Houses were covered with excrement and waste. He wondered how it had accumulated in the short time since he had last visited. As he looked around, he began to understand.

He saw the people working hard for little in return, and when they challenged, they were beaten. Their frustration and desperation oozed from their pores into the streets like a thick sludge.

'Where previously they had governed openly and honestly, everything now seemed shrouded in secrecy. The suspicions floated into the atmosphere, smearing the houses with a thick, foul-smelling substance.'

Jeda could picture the very scene. She imagined their faces and thought how helpless they must feel. She felt pity for the chief, as these were his friends, but at least he had the chance of saving his own people from this hell.

'The chief tried to find the elders who had once governed this village, but every attempt to travel or to enter a building, even to speak to someone in charge, was met with endless obstacles and pointless tasks to complete. He was tired and, like the others, his exhaustion dropped in beads of sweat, creating a foul, stinking river of slime and grease that began to penetrate the foundations of the homes.

'The chief believed that the relationships with other villages must still exist, but the strangers had created new networks: when gifts arrived for the people, they had to first pass through the governing bodies.'

Jeda suspected the villagers would see nothing of these gifts.

'Actually, they did see something of those gifts,' said the old woman, as if seeing into Jeda's mind. 'The wrappers and waste and all that remained of them flowed towards their houses in a flood of sewage and began to pile high against their homes. The stench was unbearable, and yet the chief saw these mountains of rubbish were home to many, who would sift through it in the hope there was something to salvage. The chief was deeply troubled.'

'He had reason to be,' Jeda said, alarmed.

'More than you think, child.'

'What do you mean, Grandmother?'

'He knew that the people were lost. You can remove a ruler, but it is much harder to regain a soul.'

'He felt the people had lost their souls?'

'They had the gifts of the forest and the rivers, ancient knowledge flowed through their veins, and yet he saw them scrabbling in piles of waste. It was a hard thing for him to see.'

'What did he do?'

'He couldn't bear it any longer. He raced home as quickly as he could, determined to throw the strangers out at any cost. However, when he arrived he saw that they had already moved into his home. They had constructed a small, shabby house for him and his family on the outskirts of the village. He was outraged and tried to fight his way back in, but the strangers were powerful, holding weapons unlike any that he had ever seen. His efforts were futile.'

'They can't just take his home,' Jeda interrupted. 'You can't just move into somebody else's house!'

'Wrong,' the old woman replied. 'When you have power and greed, you can do whatever you like! That is what the chief discovered. He saw the laws and systems that held his community together quickly dismantled, with new ones taking their place. He realised they were the worst kind of thieves. Not the opportunistic ones who pluck bread from a stall or a gold coin from a pocket. No, these were thieves of dreams, opportunities and dignity, who offer nothing in return. The change was too quick and the results were obvious. When he saw the pitiful wages offered to his people for their hard labour, the chief knew that something had to be done to protect his family and his friends. He needed to pacify the strangers and so he requested a meeting.'

'Good! I am glad he is taking action!' Jeda stated, imbued with a sense of righteousness.

'What do you think took place at that meeting?' the old woman asked.

'Well, I guess . . .' Jeda started. 'I guess he would have insisted on making sure the people were safe. That they were treated well. Maybe even that they had plenty to eat. The basics, really.'

'You are right!'

A small smile of satisfaction passed over Jeda's lips.

'That is exactly what he asked for. Protection of his lands and good treatment of his people. But the strangers wanted something in return.'

Jeda's smile faded.

'They agreed to his request on the condition that he prove his loyalty to them and only then would he be rewarded with land and herds of cattle. He asked how he would be expected to prove his loyalty. Their response called into question everything that he knew about himself.'

Jeda shifted uncomfortably.

'They asked for a bird.'

'A bird!' Jeda exclaimed. She was relieved, as she had expected to hear something much worse.

'Not any bird, child. In every village here, you will find an extremely rare and special bird who forms an unbreakable bond with that community. Some say the bird is gifted straight from God! All I know is that the colour of its feathers form a rich tapestry that speaks to every event that takes place in the community. The bird would open its beak and its sweet voice would sing of ancient battles. It knew the lineage of every member of the society. And the elders of each village would request its presence at moments of celebration or mourning, for when it arrived it would recite the names of their heroes and heroines and remind them who they were.'

And, of course, the chief knew where their bird would be! Jeda thought to herself. She was concerned. The bird seemed incredibly precious to the community. 'Grandmother, please tell me he did not give it to them!'

'They did not ask to keep it. They wished merely to see it.'

'Obviously it's a trick!' Jeda rolled her eyes.

The old woman shrugged and smiled sadly. 'I cannot say what went through his mind. Perhaps he was desperate. Perhaps he hoped that just one tiny little peek would satisfy them and things would return to how they were. So he agreed.'

•   •   •

Jeda was stunned. She couldn't believe what she was hearing. Surely, the chief would see sense and find a different way. But the old woman continued.

'The chief stooped as he entered the tiny house, cursing as he bashed his head on the doorframe. His heart was heavy, veering from doubt to hope. He had to do something. He gathered up his snares and headed out into the forest. He arrived at a clearing he had visited many times before, then looked around, before calling for the bird. Several moments passed in silence, but the bird did not come. The chief knew that it could only be summoned in moments of great importance, so he decided to lay down his snares, for at least they never failed him. He prayed for success in trapping the bird, then went home and waited.'

Jeda was frustrated. She understood the difficult position the chief found himself in, and yet the promise of the good things to come seemed hard to believe. What else could he do? She remembered when she was twelve years old. Things were difficult at home and she was so frustrated that she had packed a suitcase, determined to find a better life with people who understood her. Aunty had caught her.

At the time she was so utterly convinced that she could leave all her problems behind, and yet Aunty had somehow persuaded her to stay. 'How can you catch a black bird at midnight, when it is not there?' she had said. Although she suspected Aunty's words were important, Jeda did not really understand their meaning at the time. What she did know was that she didn't want to leave Aunty behind. She wondered now about the consequences of her decision, had she decided not to listen, and whether the chief might have wondered too.

She was lost in thought when she noticed the old woman had stopped telling the tale.

'Continue, Grandmother.'

The old woman nodded.

'The next morning he left to collect the bird from the snare, but, to his shock, the traps were empty. This had never happened to him before, and in a state of disbelief he picked up the snares and moved to a new part of the forest. Once again, he placed them down, then returned home and waited. For the next few hours he anxiously paced up and down, silently mouthing prayers that he would trap the bird. His wife Aziza noticed how stressed he was and came to ask after him, but he rebuked her and sent her on her way. She had many things weighing on her mind, so left him to his own concerns. The following morning he went to retrieve the traps.'

'And? Did he catch the bird?' Jeda asked uneasily.

The old woman looked down at her feet. Then slowly she shook her head.

'No, he did not. He found nothing, not a monkey, not a rabbit, not a fowl. Nothing! It was as though the entire world was against him. Everything that he had worked towards was gone. Those he considered friends could not be trusted. Some did nothing to help remedy the situation and others, he now suspected, worked for the strangers. Then this! His one chance of securing a future for his family appeared to be a complete waste of time. His throat was dry. His chest tightened. He wondered if he had somehow wronged the ancestors and this was retribution.'

Jeda was not sure if she felt sorry for him or not. How do you fix an upside-down world when you can trust nobody?

The story went on.

'The chief went to the furthest reaches of the forest. He placed the traps down, then threw himself to his knees. He raised his arms high to the sky and, overcome with emotion, trembling and shaking, he spoke to his gods and wept. He begged them for kindness and understanding. He begged them for forgiveness, for having allowed things to reach this point. He prayed that his mother would absolve him of sin, that because of all she had endured, all she had fought and struggled for, she of all people would understand. He prayed for his wife Aziza to overcome her desperate sadness. He prayed that his sons would find strength to restore order. He prayed until he could not speak any more, then he went home and waited.

'Several hours later he returned, only to find the first snare empty. The second was the same. The third and the fourth held nothing, but in the fifth something moved.'

HOW MUCH FOR
A PRICELESS BIRD?

Jeda could feel her heart pounding in her chest.

'It's not a good thing!' she said. 'They will steal it from him.' Jeda prayed that there was still a tiny chance that the chief would not go through with it.

But the voice of the old woman went on.

'Chief Bohero narrowed his eyes as he approached, keen to see if he had succeeded, and when he saw the rich colours, vibrant and gleaming, his soul leapt for joy.

'The bird was more beautiful than he remembered. It gazed up at him trustingly. He carefully lifted it from the trap and wrapped it in a small cloth, then gently placed it in his bag. He took it back to the village. On the way, he wondered where he might hide it so that nobody would see it and condemn his actions. His plan was to show it to the strangers and then release it back into the forest, and nobody would be any the wiser. His mother's sight had failed her in recent years and he had insisted that she live with them. Her house would be empty, so he headed there.'

'I hope the bird sang loudly and let everyone know what he was about to do!' cried Jeda angrily.

'What if this was the only way you could secure your family's future? Would you not do the same?' came the old woman's reply.

Jeda didn't know. She wanted to believe that she would find another way, a better way, so she remained silent as the story went on.

'The chief took the long route to his mother's house, avoiding eye contact with the few people that he met along the way. He moved quickly, aware that the bird could make a sound at any moment and give him away. He saw the little house through some bushes, so he quickened his pace. He arrived, pushed open the door and made his way in, closing the door behind him. The little house was small and dark, but it was comfortable and held everything that his mother had ever needed.

'As his eyes became accustomed to the dim light, he noticed a small cage high up on a shelf. It was perfect! He opened the little door, then, taking the bird from his bag, he held it up and gently placed it inside. He saw how the bird looked at him questioningly, moving its little head from side to side in short, sharp movements, but he could not bring himself to look it in the eye. He searched around for some grain.'

'At least he's taking care of it,' mumbled Jeda, trying to find the positive in the story.

'Yes. The bird was very precious to him and he wanted it in perfect condition, so when he saw that there was no grain in his mother's house, he decided to leave the house and get some. He did not realise that his mother was slowly making her way to her old house.'

'That's great!' cried Jeda. 'She will find the bird there, release it and save it.'

'The chief's mother had once been a formidable leader – Chief Mekati. She was wise and, despite being unable to see, she noticed many things. She had sensed the tension. The family had gone through so much – grieving the loss of a daughter, being forced off their land, and now they were in danger of losing everything. She had once fought battles and led armies, but the only thing she could offer was advice and love. She returned to her home to collect some secret ingredients to bring courage and wisdom into their home. She made her way slowly but surely, feeling her way with her carved walking stick, her heart celebrating the small victories of independence along the way.

'She reached the little earthen home and entered, stopping for a while to allow the familiar scents to wash over her. She headed directly to a corner and began to collect the gourds that held all manner of powders and liquids. All of a sudden she sensed she was not alone. Her ears listened for the tiniest sound, her nose twitching to detect anything that did not belong. The bird was still, watching her as it stood in the cage, but just then it ruffled its feathers. The old blind woman recognised the sound and immediately headed towards it.'

Yes, thought Jeda to herself. She couldn't wait for the story to end. She had it pictured so clearly. Chief Mekati would free the bird and it would fly off into the forest, where it would be safe for many years to come. Chief Bohero would have to find another way to save his people. Everybody would gather together and, using their skills and their strength, they would fight alongside each other to push the strangers out of their village and peace would return.

'The old woman's fingers fumbled in the dark as she found the cage and tried to open the latch. Wary that the bird may try to escape, she gripped it tightly by the legs. The bird did not sing and, unable to see the beauty of its feathers that revealed the stories of her people, she did not realise the nature of the bird.

'Chief Mekati remembered the last time her son had left a guinea fowl in the cage. He was planning on gifting it to his wife in an attempt to brighten her spirits. While he himself loved to prepare meals, he had a fondness for his mother's cuisine and for her help. The old woman had prepared a delicious meal of guinea fowl stew, with a spicy rich tomato sauce and a staple with flour that she had ground herself so fine it was like dust. She knew of their love for the fruit of the mabuyu tree and had coated the little white seeds in a sugary syrup with a deliciously fiery ingredient. Aziza had been more like her old joyous self for several weeks afterwards.'

Jeda did not want to hear it. 'Grandmother, this is not how to end the story.'

'The story has only just begun. With a toothless smile, the old warrior queen Mekati decided to prepare a delicious stew for her son and his wife. So intent on plucking the soft feathers from its neck to ensure death came swiftly, she did not notice an insignificant little brown bird come and sit by the doorway, anxiously peering in. She took a knife . . .'

Jeda sat with bated breath. She knew it couldn't possibly happen.

'. . . she raised it, and with warrior speed she sliced off the head. As she chopped the warm flesh into pieces, seasoned them and placed them in a pot, before tidying the feathers away, she did not see the soul of the bird slowly floating towards the doorway. She

did not see the little brown bird spread its wings and open its beak, receiving this special gift. She did not see the sudden change of its feathers as they took on the flashes of colour that told of battles and triumphs, marriages and deaths, disasters and wars. She did not see the little bird fly away back to the forest.'

'Wait!' Jeda cried. 'You mean the bird did not die?'

'The bird knew it was going to die, but it needed its soul to live on. Some things are too valuable! Mekati focused on preparing her meal and realised that there was one ingredient missing. She left the house and proceeded to feel her way to the section of her farm where a certain type of chilli grew. This chilli was sweet and fiery, adding a delightful kick to every meal. She wanted this meal to be perfect for her son and his wife.'

Jeda's face held a horrified expression, but she leaned in to hear more. The old storyteller watched her with squinted eyes.

'What do you think happened next?'

'The chief returned,' Jeda replied.

'Yes, the chief returned. He immediately saw the cage door open. The bird had gone. He was aghast! How could this be? He crawled on the ground, calling out for the bird in the faint hope that it had released itself, but to no avail. He stood still and was filled with an intense rage. This bird would guarantee a future for him and his family. This bird was everything and somebody had the audacity to steal it from him. He needed to do something. He reckoned that returning to the forest was his only possibility. He hoped he could find a bird that was similar in some way, so that he may be able to trick the strangers. He snatched up his snares and stormed out of the little house towards the forest. He did not see his mother hunched over her vegetable patch, selecting the sweetest chillies she could find.'

'Did she see him or hear him? What happened next? Tell me!' Jeda begged.

'Patience, patience,' the old woman said, stretching out her legs.

'Chief Bohero ventured deeper into the forest. The canopy of trees appeared to curve towards him, as though trying to provide protection. His eyes sought out any flash of colour, any clue as to the whereabouts of a beautiful bird that could pass. He opened his throat and uttered a variety of sweet melodies in a bid to attract movement, but none came. As the hours passed, he realised his window of opportunity was soon closing and he needed to find the bird. He dropped to the ground and raised his arms to the heavens, praying. He begged those who had gone before to show him the way. He picked up handfuls of sharp stones and thorns and crushed them in his hands, watching his blood drip to the ground in a simple sacrifice. He promised that he just needed this one favour and he would do whatever they wanted.

'I am not sure if they decided to help or if he was simply fortunate, but just then there was a flash of colour in the branches overhead. The chief looked upwards and a little bird opened its beak and began to chirrup loudly. It sang praises of his family's name and the mighty deeds they had accomplished. The chief was speechless. He stretched out a hand and the bird flew onto it. He quickly placed it into his bag and headed straight for the strangers.'

'Grandmother, it doesn't make sense,' Jeda chimed in, clearly annoyed. 'If the bird knew what he was going to do, why would it help him?'

'It may not make sense to you, but everything has its time, even though the results may not be seen for hundreds of years.'

•　　•　　•

Jeda pondered the old woman's words, before the rickety voice spoke on.

'The chief stood before a council of strangers, with his bag by his side. "Do you have it?" they asked. "Yes," he replied.

'He placed the bag gently on the ground and had just started to open it when he paused. He raised his head and questioned, "Just a look, right?" They smiled at him. "Just a look." He opened the bag and gently took out the bird and raised it towards them.'

Jeda felt sick. She knew deep inside her that this was very wrong, but despite her fears she longed to know more.

'The council approached him, their eyes wide and eager. They reached out their fingers to touch the bird, but the chief resisted. "Only a look," he reminded them. They crowded around him and he began to feel extremely uncomfortable. They pressed him, "Come on, just one touch. We will give you more land."

'He heard the honey-coated words repeating over again. "Just a touch." He considered how much influence and power he stood to gain. He knew his family would be secure. He thought that over time he would be able to return the village to its former glory, so he agreed. He allowed their grubby fingers to caress the shimmering feathers of the bird, but the more they touched, the greedier they became. They wanted more. Their desire overcame them. Each one wanted to hold the precious bird, so they tried to prise it from his hands.'

'No! They will hurt it!' Jeda cried, horrified, as her imagination played out the scene in front of her.

The old woman could not stop.

'They did. Even though Chief Bohero held on, they grabbed at the bird's wings. They pulled hard, ripping the feathers out of its flesh. The bird cried out in agony. The chief began to shout, but his words were drowned out, as they screamed, "Get the bird. Give us the bird! We must have it!" Grasping hands tore at it. Delicate feathers that had lost their gleam fell to the floor. A snapping sound indicated the birds legs had been broken. It desperately tried to flee, managing to find a gap in the throng, and with a final push it broke away, leaving fistfuls of feathers in the strangers' hands.'

The old woman stopped speaking and sighed softly. The heart-breaking shrieks of the little bird resounded in Jeda's mind and she was tortured by the image.

'How could the chief do that?'

The old woman's gnarled and crooked fingers scratched at her legs. 'He wondered the same thing too.'

'I hope he never finds peace. I hope that they betray him and make him suffer,' Jeda cried angrily.

'They didn't have to do very much at all. He carried that burden himself. No weight is heavier than a man's own shame.

'The chief saw the bird fly into a nearby thorn bush and drag itself along the ground to safety. Its vibrant colours were a poor reflection of its former glory, every inch smeared with blood. He reached out a hand and called gently, but the bird refused to approach him. He was filled with guilt. The history of his world was broken and he was responsible. The strangers' offer of land was stained with blood and he now fully understood their intentions. But as he wondered if there was still time to leave and join the rebels in destroying the newcomers' increasingly numerous strongholds, they asked for his help. They wanted him to keep the peace and prove his loyalty. They promised more land if he did. Without knowing why, the chief found himself agreeing.'

'What a coward! Surely they now know he will do anything they ask.'

'Of course. They praised him and welcomed him into their fold. They grinned and asked if he might help them find the rebels to negotiate a truce.'

'Surely he can't trust them!'

Jeda immediately thought of Aunty, who when she disapproved of something would say, 'Ehe, you are moving from a hornet's nest to the jaws of a crocodile.'

'The chief could not refuse. He was a traitor, but in truth he had no information. To be of value, he knew he had to give them something. He thought of the bird. He had placed it in the cage in secrecy. Nobody had seen him. Unless, of course, he had been followed. Yes, that was it! The idea began to grow in his mind, so much so that he started to believe it himself. He went to the council and announced, "My friends, earlier someone tried to steal the bird from me. The person who stole the bird must be a rebel." Immediately, the strangers set off.'

Jeda said nothing but swallowed hard.

'I can stop here, child,' the old woman said.

Jeda remembered her mother's words: 'You must be loyal to the story.' She shook her head.

'Then I will go on. The strangers headed straight to where the bird had been stolen. The chief sat in the plush surroundings, awaiting their return. It wasn't long before they found his mother and demanded to know if she had taken the bird. Of course she had! She thought of the delicious meal she planned to cook for her son and proudly confessed. They immediately threw her to the ground and tied her arms behind her back. Her cries attracted the attention of the villagers, who raced over to help her. They were horrified to see their grandmother, their hero, their warrior queen, Chief Mekati, a woman whose feats were sung across the kingdom, being subjected to such barbaric behaviour. They tried to reach her, to save her, but their blades and sticks were no match for the weapons of the strangers. Held down with a baton, they demanded to know the whereabouts of the other rebels.

'The old, blind woman told them she did not know, so they dragged her to a tree and placed a noose around her neck. They forced her onto a small, wobbly stool and again tried to prise information from her. She remained silent, so with a leather strap they whipped her, tearing shreds of skin from her wrinkled body until finally they announced they would push her off her stand unless she spoke.

'She was blind, but she could hear the helpless screams of the villagers around her, so she used her final breath to utter the words: "Tell them nothing!"

'She swung for several hours before they allowed her people to cut her down.'

·   ·   ·

Jeda had nothing to say.

After a long period, the old woman started to rise up.

'Wait, Grandmother. How does it end?'

'It has not yet ended. You saw the village. You saw what the chief left for his people. When he saw his mother's lifeless body, he was consumed with such guilt that he believed he was truly broken, damaged beyond redemption. He did not realise that even after everything he could have still found forgiveness and made amends.

'But, child, listen. The bird continues to live. Some speak of its ugly feathers, its broken legs and fragile wings. They ask what possible value this bruised and broken bird can hold. But there are many of us who know. Many who believe. And remember, everything has its time.'

The old woman struggled to her feet and started to move away.

'Grandmother!' Jeda called after her, but the woman simply raised her stick, waved it in the air and continued without a backward glance.

WHERE A FATHER
FINDS HIS DAUGHTER

'Jeda! Jeda!' A voice rang out around her and, shaken out of a stupor, she awoke to find her father standing over her, a concerned look on his face.

'Jeda. Are you okay? Aunty told me you were lost in a story and I came in to find you passed out. What's going on?'

She closed her eyes for several minutes, then after she had come to her senses her father insisted on making her a cup of cocoa. It was something he hadn't done in many years. Although Jeda didn't really want one, she understood that this was his way of showing her that he loved and cared for her, and so she accepted gratefully. She held the warm drink in her hand.

Chris sat opposite her and wondered at how big she had become. *When did that happen?* She was so beautiful and smart, and yet he realised he didn't know very much about her at all. He began to question what kind of father he had become, if he had let her down. Had he done enough? Was he able to give her what she needed? Aunty was now her mother figure, but was she enough? Did his daughter miss her mother still? Of course she missed her mother. It was a silly thought and he chided himself.

'Do you want to tell me about the story?' he asked gently, waiting for the inevitable negative response.

Jeda was about to shrug her shoulders and tell him that he wouldn't understand, but for some reason she decided to tell him. She explained how inadequate she had believed herself to be. How lonely she had felt. She told him about meeting the Shadowman on the mountain, about opening the box, about her family, her feelings of belonging. She told him everything, and even though he didn't understand much of it, he realised it was important to her and he listened.

He raised his eyebrows as she explained how the Shadow had slashed her and Aunty had stepped into the story and saved her. He was impressed at how rich and complex this world she had created appeared to be, but he was equally concerned that if she continued to believe in it as she seemed to, then it might take her away from the real world. He briefly wondered if he knew any psychologists who might be able to offer advice or help.

When she finished, he held her hand. 'Thank you, sweetheart. I really appreciate you opening up to me like that.'

Jeda saw that it may have been too much for him to handle and made a move to stand up. He seized her hand again and she sat back down.

'Jeda, I think we should talk about this. I know you miss the stories your mother told you, but you do know they are just stories, right?'

'Dad, they are not just stories. They are real. I've been there. I've seen them.'

'Look I'm not saying they aren't important . . .' he started.

She shook her head, regretting that she had revealed so much of herself to him. Of course he wouldn't understand. He never had. 'They are more than important. They are everything.'

Her father felt his blood beginning to surge through his veins. He was annoyed. Every time they had a conversation she would refuse to listen. Time and time again! He knew that she wouldn't respond to his frustration, so he simplified things right down.

'Sweetheart, your mother was the most wonderful woman. She gave you stories that have inspired your beautiful, wonderful imagination and I love how much you want to believe in them.' Her father smiled softly, as he took her face in his hands and looked at her tenderly. 'But, Jeda, you have to understand that these are just stories. They have no connection to the real world.'

Jeda's brow crumpled. She knew the power of the stories. She had felt their effect on her. They had changed everything she knew. She wanted her father to understand.

'The Shadowman is in me. He is in you.'

She saw him roll his eyes.

'Dad, if you just listen to—'

'Jeda, stop! The Shadow is a story! It doesn't exist.'

'But . . .'

'Enough!' He looked furious.

But Jeda was angry too. She grabbed hold of his hand and she opened the box. Immediately, the stories rushed free and swirled around them. She saw a look of confusion in her father's eyes, lit up by the gold and silver swirls. He was fearful. His eyes darted around, trying to understand what was going on. His hand gripped hers so tight his knuckles turned pure white.

Jeda smiled calmly.

'Dad, it's okay.'

And they were gone.

• • •

The transition into the story took a fraction of a second. Jeda and her father found themselves in the middle of a desert. The sun was blinding. They both squinted hard, raising their hands to protect their eyes. It was scorching hot, with a brilliant blue sky above them and endless golden dunes rising and falling around them, the tiny sand particles dancing in spirals as the wind picked them up and toyed with them.

'What's happening?' cried Chris, breathing hard as he tried to make sense of everything.

Jeda did not reply. She knew there was no answer she could give that would satisfy him at that moment. She clambered to the top of the tallest sand dune and strained to see any form of life. Her father clambered up after her, sweating profusely.

As the two stood gazing outwards, their backs to the sun, the particles of sand hovered like a great barricade before them, separating them from the world beyond. Then without warning, the winds dropped and the sand crumbled to the ground, revealing a hidden entrance to an enchanting little village. Small, square houses dotted the scene like golden sugar cubes shimmering under the honeyed rays of the sun. Men and women in flowing robes of all colours milled past each other, moving so slowly and gracefully across the sands that Jeda imagined they were gliding. On their heads they bore baskets filled with an array of goods.

'Wow!' her father's voice interrupted her thoughts. Jeda glanced at him before careening down the slope at full speed. Her father was hesitant, but Jeda yelled, 'Let's go!' He was unwilling to be left behind, so he launched a frantic scramble to reach the bottom of the dune.

As they began the walk to the village, the voice of Jeda's mother filled their ears.

'There was once a wife and her husband.'

'Is that your—' Chris started.

'Ssshhh,' replied Jeda.

As Chris listened to his wife, his eyes began to glisten as distant memories came flooding back to him. The voice that had once soothed and encouraged him, that had whispered sweet things to him, now surrounded him. It was so soft, but with such depth that it entered every part of him and he trembled uncontrollably. How could he have forgotten such beauty?

'They lived in a land where the sand shimmered like a sheen of gossamer. The blue of the sky radiated peace and the sun rose every day with such brilliance that from a distance you would think this was truly heaven on earth.'

As he gazed at the rich beauty around him, Chris remembered that Rahami's words had always brought worlds to life.

'But there was a poison in this land. A clear, invisible poison. It travelled through the air and when it sensed an individual's movement into power it would pass from breath to breath. Once transmitted, it would begin to take hold. It would navigate through the blood vessels, heading straight for the core. The recipient of the poison would first feel an exhilaration, but after some time they would be filled with a sense of doubt. Soon after, a

143

sense of helplessness would engulf them and they would feel incapable of fulfilling what they had set out to achieve. Their eyes would see misery and injustice, but their hearts would be blind to it.

'The poison allowed them to believe that somehow they were invincible and, as they were surrounded by others who had also been infected, they would find comfort in each other. Eventually, even those who resisted would lose the capacity to fight the poison and it would settle deep in their souls, slowly transmitting through their families. The poison was so wily, so insidious, that the recipient would not realise they were infected until they were entirely stripped of their humanity and compassion.'

Jeda looked around. She saw the beautiful faces of the people, some laughing, others deep in conversation. She tried to see who might have been poisoned. It was very hard to tell. Her father must have been thinking the same thing, as he whispered to her, 'Do you think it has passed to anyone here?'

'They can't hear you, Dad. Nobody can see you here. You are a ghost to them.'

Her father looked around, seeing that this was indeed true.

Rahami continued her story.

'The husband sold bread in the marketplace. He was loved, for he was kind to everyone. If anyone was hungry and could not afford even a slice, he would ensure they got something to eat. In the evenings he would return home, where his wife had prepared a delicious meal, and they would joke and laugh with each other until they both fell asleep. After a few years of marriage, the wife and the husband were blessed with a son. He was an extraordinary child, born of starlight. His lips sparkled. His skin glowed. His eyes twinkled, reflecting the planets, the universe, the infinite. As they held him, they knew that he was a very special child.'

Just then, Chris noticed a tall man with a beaming smile selling a variety of breads and rolls from a stall and indicated to Jeda that perhaps this was the husband. He was surrounded by men and women, each one holding up a small coin, eager to leave with bread for the body and a story for the soul. He was clearly a man who loved his work. At his feet they noticed a tiny boy darting in and out of people's legs, wild with curiosity. He seemed to have inherited his father's love of life. The light in his eyes was so brilliant that neither Jeda nor her father could look away from him. He was beautiful. The two watched for hours until finally, as the sun began to set, the husband packed up his baskets and shut up shop, scooping the little boy into his arms and carrying him high on his shoulders, as they headed home.

Jeda and Chris watched as the boy grew under the watchful eye of his parents, who laughed as he somersaulted through the village with his friends; they taught him hospitality, kindness and cooperation; they encouraged his stubbornness, unless it was a danger to himself.

'I was once like that,' his father had declared. 'And I turned out quite well.'

They witnessed the boy's pride at winning a race in school and the guilt he felt for not helping his mother, who, having forgotten to kneel when armed soldiers approached, cowered on the floor trying to shield herself from the blows inflicted on her with wooden truncheons.

They were delighted at his joy when they welcomed a baby girl into their family. They were amused by his often tender yet hysterical perspective of the world, which he shared with the customers at the bread stall, where he learnt his father's trade. They saw how he tried to navigate his way through a world, filled with fear and worry, while trying to be responsible. There were moments Jeda recognised all too well, for the young boy was struggling with a voice inside him, just as she had. She suspected it was his own Shadowman.

Jeda rested her head on her father's shoulder as they set in for the night. The house was bustling, with the wife busy preparing the evening meal with help from two visiting sisters. Her grandfather sat half asleep to the great amusement of the children, who sneakily tried to wake him up by tickling his chin with a blade of grass, and the husband was preparing to regale his family with stories of his experiences that day. With the meal ready, the wife called for them to come and try out her delicious new recipes, to which there was no hesitation.

'This tomato sauce tastes like heaven!' the father cried out.

'Mama, you are the best cook in the world!' the boy shouted excitedly, as he served himself a second, then a third helping.

'Nobody in the world can prepare such perfect bread!' one of the wife's sisters exclaimed, as she broke apart the round, flat delicacies.

'If only you would teach me!' her other sister mumbled through a mouthful of stuffed peppers and spicy herbs.

'Some things can only come from the heart!' the wife replied, and she continued to heap out mountains of food until nobody could eat any more and they lay helpless but happy.

Her love of food had been passed down the generations and there was no ingredient that she could not turn into a delicious meal. She was aware that this gift was an important part of her family's experiences together, so she treasured every moment. As he saw the happiness on their faces, Chris wondered what special routines he shared with Jeda. Annoyingly, he couldn't think of one and squeezed her tight as he realised he needed to make time for some.

Rahami's voice echoed around them.

'As the child grew, his parents realised how smart he was. How quickly he learnt new skills and how his heart swelled with compassion and determination to help others. They began to consider that perhaps he was one of the Wasanaa, a group of special children born with the intention to help rid the land of the poison. The more they considered it, the more they believed it to be true. They had never met one of the Wasanaa before, but he appeared to have all the qualities required. They studied him closely, continuously testing him, because they needed to be sure. To become a Wasanaa required a great sacrifice from the family. The child would need to obtain certain skills, knowledge and experience that was simply not possible in their own land. But there was a place. The Land in the Sky . . .'

THE LAND IN THE SKY

Jeda loved the sound of it: the Land in the Sky.

She said the phrase several times, allowing it to circulate around her mouth. *The Land in the Sky.* In her mind, she conjured up images of high castles nestled between bright blue mountains. She could picture magnificent buildings poking out between woolly white clouds, a place of peace.

'It sounds wonderful!' she sighed.

'Yes,' her father agreed.

Rahami's voice interrupted their thoughts.

'*The boy's parents, indeed his entire family, had heard many stories of this place. They spoke often of it. How beautiful it was, its opulence, opportunities at every turn. It was a good place. A just place, where knowledge and skill were valued more than gold. Where even the lowliest citizen was treated with dignity and honour. However, reaching the Land in the Sky came at a great cost. Not only was the journey fraught with danger, there were many obstacles along the way. It was hard and tough, and many did not survive. However, as the boy grew, so did the parents' determination to send him there, so they saved every piece of gold they could and every day they prayed for blessings and goodwill upon him.*'

Jeda and her father watched as they nurtured the boy, preparing him for the destiny they believed to be his. They told him stories of how life was before the poison had arrived. They painted pictures in his soul and he longed to play a role in returning the land to its former glory. They watched his courage grow as he re-enacted scenarios where he was invincible, a crusader fighting an invisible foe. Every night when he fell asleep, his dreams were so vivid; he truly believed that his reason for existing was to be in service to others and his character was such that he was determined to take on the challenge.

'I wish I knew my purpose,' Jeda reflected thoughtfully.

'You are still young.'

'Did you always know yours?'

'I thought I did. Then I lost it for a bit. But it's coming back,' her father replied with a smile, as he squeezed her hand. They followed the boy as he grew into a young man, full of respect and love for his parents.

'*The day arrived when the boy's parents felt the time had come,*' Rahami's rich voice spoke. '*But when they counted their savings, they realised it would not be enough. They needed help and so they gathered their neighbours and relatives. They told them of their intention, and those who believed the boy had the strength, talent and will to succeed, and who saw in him a better future, were happy to sacrifice what gold they had. His parents sold their lands, confident he would succeed in his quest and they would all be better off.*

'*They summoned their son. His father gave him the small bag of gold, laid his hand on his head and wished him every blessing. His mother filled a bag with niceties, and reminded him of his responsibilities. With tears in her eyes, she insisted he send regular messages home to inform them of how he was keeping. With these words in his head, he embarked on his journey.'*

Jeda and her father immediately set off after the handsome young man. He moved with great strides, so it was an effort to keep up. His robes billowed in the desert winds, but this was his land, so he knew how to protect his eyes and nose from the elements.

He strode across the shimmering sands, heading towards the distant hills. As he approached, he saw these were no hills but great jagged mountains and he had no choice but to climb over them. Jeda and her father scrambled up after him, skidding on the precarious scree, bruising themselves and nursing their bleeding feet in the evenings as they rested. The young man would always light a fire to keep away the wild animals and then lie down and gaze up at the stars, dreaming of what lay ahead.

After three days of intense and brutal mountaineering, they began the descent and relief overcame them all. Their joy was short-lived, however, as they came to a mighty river. There appeared to be no way across. The water foamed and swirled, crashing over gigantic rocks, carrying enormous logs from upstream.

'What can we do?' Jeda asked desperately.

The young man looked upstream and walked a few hundred metres, then turned and walked in the other direction, trying to see if the water appeared calm at any point. But unfortunately it was impossible to tell: the raging river stretched as far as the eye could see.

'The young man with the dazzling eyes remembered the stories he had been told and knew that sometimes he would have to look beyond what lay in front of him. He scanned the horizon, concentrating hard, and then he

saw it. Across the river on the far bank, over to the west, he could just make out a thin rope reaching down from the heavens. He smiled.'

'Yes! He found the rope,' Chris yelled out joyfully.

'The Land in the Sky, here we come!' Jeda hooted happily.

Jeda was leaping around with excitement until she realised what the young man intended to do.

·   ·   ·

Knowing he needed to get to the other side of the river, the young man tested the speed of the water, measuring the current and estimating the distance to the other side.

'Dad, he is going to swim across!' Jeda cried out.

'He can't! He'll never make it,' Chris exclaimed.

Rahami's rich voice pushed them closer to the river.

'The young man needs to cross. He realised that if he launched himself towards a certain point, he would enter a clear flow where he would avoid being smashed against the rocks. The flow would carry him towards the opposite shore, and if he timed it correctly he saw a point downstream where, with some considerable effort, he might be able to pull himself out of the current. There was no choice. He tied his belongings tight against his body and then proceeded to the bank.'

The rush of water was frightening. Jeda saw him looking up and down, in one last-ditch attempt to spot an alternative route, but there was none. This was it.

'Go upstream a little further. It is bound to narrow,' Jeda shouted over the sound of the water, but he was oblivious to her cries. 'You'll never make it out!' she pleaded.

But it was no use. The young man waited for a log to pass and he leapt in. He was immediately sucked into the furious current and he waved his arms wildly, struggling to keep his head above the water, but it wasn't long before he disappeared from view.

Chris immediately raced along the shore, trying to catch sight of him, but it was no use. The water was too powerful. He saw it was futile and stopped, resting his hands on his knees and trying to catch his breath. He turned to seek out Jeda, but to his horror he saw her launch herself into the water after the man.

'No!' he wailed.

His fear of losing Jeda overcame his fear of the waves and, without any hesitation, he too jumped in. On the surface, there was no sign of any soul, but under the water a battle for survival was taking place. The young man tried desperately to right himself, as the water forced him to tumble, and as he stabilised he was able to swim to the surface. His lungs felt like they were about to explode. He was a man of the desert and not of the water, but he had to try.

Bubbles blowing in all directions confused both Chris and Jeda, and they struggled to make sense of which way was up, but they succeeded and soon three little heads appeared on the surface. The current was fierce, pushing them downstream at tremendous speed, then suddenly the young man noticed a change in the current. As the river raged around a bend, the section of flow in which he found himself slowed right down and he knew this was his chance. With a huge effort he used every ounce of strength to free himself from the mighty suction and swam to the bank, where he pulled himself up and collapsed, panting heavily.

Jeda and her father were terrified as they tried to keep their heads above water. It was cold and fast-moving. It roared so loudly they could not hear each other speak. But as they approached the tight bend, Chris knew that he needed to get out. He kicked off against a rock, which pulled him free from the current, and he managed to find his feet in the shallows just in time to grab Jeda's hand and yank her to safety. They were desperate to rest but noticed the young man stand up and head towards the rope.

They followed after him as Rahami's voice began.

'*The rope hung loose and was so long that it disappeared into the clouds, but, ignoring how the wet clothes clung to his skin, the young man readied himself, gripped the rope and began to climb upwards.*

But the Land in the Sky does not accept people too easily. When they saw him approach, they sent wind and rain to knock him off the rope. As the rope swayed violently, he held on with every ounce of strength he had.'

'Don't let go!' Jeda cried from below. 'Keep climbing!'

'*When the wind and rain had eased, the young man continued to climb. But the Land in the Sky does not accept people too easily. They poured oil down the rope and, as his hands absorbed the grease, they could not hold on and he quickly began to slide. He knew he could not fail, so he seized the rope with his teeth, biting down hard. He embedded his fingernails into the rope fibres and held on so tightly he felt his fingers would break off. After a long time, he found the sun had dried the oil. He continued to climb. But the Land in the Sky does not accept people too easily. They were outraged that still he continued, and they sent hornets as large as birds. They circled around him and he tried to bat them away, gripping the rope between his knees. They stung his legs, his face, his back. He cried out in pain, but still he continued to climb. Soon he was through the clouds and he could see the gateway. This was it, he thought to himself. He had arrived.*

'But they did not want him to enter and so, as he neared the entrance, they set fire to the rope. His eyes widened in panic as he thought of how far he would fall. The rope began to fray. He could feel the fibres snapping and breaking. He thought of his father and remembered the bag. He reached into his pocket, took out the gold and held it up towards them. When they saw that delightful golden gleam, their eyes widened. They hauled the young man up and welcomed him in.'

WHEN ONE
DREAMS OF HOME

Jeda and Chris found themselves strolling behind the young man. The Land in the Sky appeared vaguely familiar to them both, as though they had walked the streets before in some dream. Magnificent old buildings towered around them, the stone blackened over time. Turrets and domes reached up to kiss the heavens. Cobblestones gave a distinct feeling of history and a time gone by, yet the city pulsed with life. Musicians could be found in every corner. Street performers breathed fire, cracked whips and attempted to humiliate grown men and women, most of whom took it in their stride, to the amusement of passers-by. Hats were passed round, filling with coins as the stories were told and the tunes were played. They looked around and saw small groups of people deep in conversation. Some were discussing the meaning of life, others were wondering what to have for dinner.

They followed the young man, his head turning this way and that, looking upon the monuments and statues which recognised the importance of knowledge and learning. Publishers were celebrated for their contributions to the literary world; great wordsmiths and poets were honoured. There was remembrance everywhere of those who had filled the city with magic and meaning. It was astounding to witness. The young man smiled. His parents had been right. This was a good place. He put his hand on the ground to create a connection between him and what would be his new world until it was time to return home. It felt right, so he whispered a message for his family.

'Mother, Father. I am well. It is good!'

'*The wind lifted the words and carried them far away from the Land in the Sky,*' came Rahami's voice. '*They travelled across rivers and mountains until finally they reached the ears of his mother, who received them with great joy.*'

Jeda was looking around the beautiful streets, when her father nudged her.

'Look!' he exclaimed.

They saw the young man enter an institution where he had enrolled himself. He knew his purpose, so he had decided to surround himself with thinkers and dreamers. These conversations, he believed, would help him narrow his focus so he could become the best man he could be. It was an exciting time for him. His eyes shone brightly. He was smart and confident and had many stories to tell, so over some time he gathered a close-knit group of friends. Some were from distant lands like his own, with dreams to create change.

Others had only ever known the Land in the Sky, but, through him, they were able to expand their horizons, as he shared stories of his upbringing and his life. Jeda noticed that when he spoke of home, his eyes filled with starlight and it was easy to become lost in them. The friends were close and spent much of their time together,

but sometimes, late at night, when the stars shone overhead, and the young man ached for his friends and family at home, he would step outside and look to the heavens. He would whisper blessings and speak stories of his adventures before asking the wind if it would carry the message home. Each time, the wind obliged.

• • •

'I have never seen someone so committed to studying,' Chris commented, as the young man sat on some steps, pulled out a book and started to read.

'What, not even me?' Jeda joked.

They laughed and Jeda became acutely aware that it was the first time she had properly laughed with her father in a long time. It was nice. If he felt the same, he never said anything, but briefly he raised his eyebrows and sighed happily as they settled back to observe the situation. It was a perfect day. The sun rose and they felt its heat warming their skin. They observed the citizens' attire immediately change from multiple layers to simple tops and shorts. Their demeanour changed, too. On cold days they moved fast with purpose, yet on the warmer days it was as though they had been granted permission to dawdle, to relax, to laugh with their companions, to greet strangers in the street. The sense of goodwill was palpable.

'*Happiness seeks out happiness,*' Rahami's voice began. '*And rather than go home and rest, the young man and his friends decided to extend their joy into the night. They decided an evening of merrymaking was in order so left their homes and headed to the liveliest part of the city. They entered a small restaurant with simple food but where a live band was scheduled to perform. They were filled with the anticipation of what would be an incredible night.*'

The sun set early and, after a bright evening, Jeda noticed how dark the night sky had become. Thick clouds had gathered, blocking out the moon and the stars. They were replaced by flickering light-bulbs that lit up the streets like some fairyland. It was utterly beautiful. They followed the young man towards the restaurant and walked in.

'*The dining space was full of life and light. Excited conversations were taking place at each table. The food orders were carried around by smartly dressed waiters. The food was not just delicious to taste but its presentation emitted gasps of wonder, as steaks sizzled on hot plates. Waiters set fire to colourful drinks that burned briefly and those brave enough downed them in seconds to the rapturous applause of their peers. The young man inhaled the rich smell of coriander and basil; the vibrant red, green and yellow colours that glistened on the plate reminded him of the dinners his mother used to make when he was young. He could almost taste her food. He raised his glass to the sky and toasted. "To a future as rich and wonderful as this meal!"*

'"*To the future!*" *they all cried in unison before starting to eat.*

'*They gnawed and chomped. They licked and chewed. They slurped and swallowed, savouring each tiny morsel, all the while topping up their glasses and laughing with joyful abandon. Suddenly the ambient music that had been playing beneath the chattering voices stopped, as the band began to set up the stage. The instruments were brought in and the entire room erupted in applause. The band waved, delighted to fill the souls present with their gift of music.'*

When the music started to play, it didn't take long for everyone to gather on the dance floor. Jeda seized her father's arm. 'Come on!'

'Jeda,' he moaned, 'I hate dancing!'

'Dad, nobody can see you, remember? What have you got to be ashamed of?'

Once his fear of shame had been removed, Jeda couldn't believe her eyes as her father spun and pirouetted between the dancers on the floor. He bent his legs, placed his hands under his armpits and proceeded to move like a chicken. Jeda laughed hysterically.

'Never do that in public!' she cried.

Chris almost bumped into the young man, whose dance moves were slow and graceful. He had an expression of serenity on his face, his eyes were closed, lost in the moment. Around him, hips jiggled, bodies swayed from side to side, smiles lit up faces as the band played tune after magical tune.

'I love this!' Jeda shrieked, as she joined in the dancing.

'Watch the young man, Jeda.' Rahami's commanding voice interrupted Jeda's mood. Jeda retreated to the edge of the dance floor. Her father joined her. They solemnly watched the young man at peace with himself. The tune changed and picked up pace and he walked to the bar for a refreshment.

'He felt as high as the sky, when suddenly across the room he caught

sight of one of the most beautiful women he had ever seen. Her hair was the colour of sunshine and her smile was as wide as the world. She was dancing with her friends and he was captivated by her.'

Jeda looked across the dancefloor and there indeed was the young woman. She had an innocence about her. As though everything around her was new. She appeared to have an open spirit and they noticed her noticing him.

'As her eyes met his, she saw the starlight pouring out of them and she thought he was perhaps the most beautiful man in the world. She smiled, a sign for him to approach, and so he did. It was not long before the young couple were smiling and laughing. They were at ease in each other's company.'

'Aha! This is a love story then!' Chris decided.

He had never been more wrong.

•   •   •

Jeda and Chris noticed they were not the only ones staring at the young couple. Across the floor, someone was watching. A young man with a furrowed brow. He sat with his elbows firmly on the table and in his right hand was a glass of golden liquid that he swirled round and round. He stared at them with such intensity that he was not aware of any other thing around him.

Jeda suddenly felt a wave of nausea overcome her. Inside, something was stirring. She could feel it. She looked around, but there was nothing untoward. Her father was watching the young couple as they danced together, the man's hand on the small of the woman's back, her hands draped over his shoulders, each one beaming.

'Dad, can you feel something?' Jeda asked.

Her father turned towards her. 'What?'

Jeda paced up and down to rid herself of the sick feeling, but it grew stronger.

The voice of Rahami broke out.

'The man was so focused on the couple that he did not see the ground begin to open up.'

Jeda swallowed hard. She knew what was coming. She looked down and beneath her the floor started to crack and crumble. She trembled as long, shadowy fingers prised their way through and emerged.

'Yes,' a voice inside her began to speak. 'Yes.'

She inhaled deeply, trying to control her breathing and desperately hoping to keep the voice silent.

'The young man with the drink,' Rahami continued, *'did not see the Shadowman creep out of the cracks, slither across the stone floor, make his way up the table leg and gently slip into his glass. The man swirled his drink once more, then peered into the bottom. That was the moment the Shadowman began to cast his spell.'*

At once, a chill overcame both Chris and Jeda.

'Dad, he is here!' she whispered.

They heard a soft, slow voice with a razor-sharp edge speak to the man as he gazed hypnotised into his glass.

'Look at them! All smiles and laughter.

'But you know his kind. You know what he's after.

'Aggressive, violent, no sense of shame.

'Always in trouble, always to blame.

'I tell you all the time – this beast.

'It wants to gorge. It wants to feast.

'It wants to take the good, the just.

'But you can stop him. Yes. You must!'

The man, emboldened by these words, knocked back his drink and stood up. He glared at the couple for a few moments before stepping forward. Jeda gripped her father's arm tightly. Chris looked up at the young couple completely lost in a moment of bliss. He turned to see the angry young man approach them, his fists clenched. Chris shook Jeda off and positioned himself alongside the man. 'What are you doing? You don't need to do this.'

But the man marched on, undeterred.

Jeda meanwhile raced towards the couple. She tried to warn them that something was about to happen. 'You've got to be careful. This guy has been watching you. Open your eyes! Open your eyes!'

She tried to knock drinks off tables, waving her arms around them. She attempted to position herself between them, but her efforts were futile.

'The young man with the furrowed brow did not see the starlight spilling from the person in front of him. There was no man, no human. In its place he saw a towering beast. Thick thighs. Thick chest. A head too big for its body.'

Chris watched, horrified, as the young man who had been dancing so gently just moments before began to transform before his eyes. He grew taller, fur sprouted from his skin. A loud rushing sound began to flood the room.

'What is going on?' he shouted.

'Get out of the way. You can't change anything,' Jeda screamed back.

There was a loud popping and the eyeballs of the beast seemed to protrude rudely from his head. His nose spread wide, giving the impression he had no cheeks at all. The enormous nostrils flared at every opportunity, emitting a foul smoke that reeked of every odious stench imaginable. He was a hideous thing that stomped and stamped, clenched fists ready to smash and crush and destroy. Every movement he made was dull and slow.

'The young man with the furrowed brow approached cautiously, as though ready for battle. Around him, a shadowy mist swirled. He sharpened words into cruel hard weapons and handed them over.'

Jeda watched with horror as the words turned into arrows and spears. She remembered the unbearable pain as they had pierced her chest that terrible day in the park. She heard the gleeful words of encouragement from the Shadowman.

'Yes, you must. Yes, you must!'

The man with the furrowed brow accepted the weaponised words and aimed them at the beast.

At that moment Rahami's voice sounded, filled with an urgency that Jeda had not heard before.

'The young man with the sparkling eyes felt the weapons pierce his skin and he whipped round to face his enemy. There, standing before him, was something more grotesque than anything he had ever imagined.'

As Jeda watched, the young man with the furrowed brow began to change. His skin blistered with foul spots that exploded, leaving hot, thick trails of pus oozing on his skin. It was a loathsome monster with hair the colour of fire. The young woman pleaded that they should stop. She screamed, but the rush in the room was so loud nobody could hear.

'The creatures approached each other. The beast saw his enemy had a hungry, determined look in his eye. He saw the twisted, crooked fingers bearing sharp talons ready to scratch and rip and tear. He saw that it was hungry for blood. Yellow strands of saliva dripped from its jaws. It snarled, revealing fangs that glinted in the moonlight. And all the while the Shadow-man gleefully danced around them, sharpening words into weapons.

'The creatures growled menacingly at each other. They circled one another, prowling. The monster seeking out that weak spot. That moment to take action. The beast ensuring he would never find it. But the moment came, and they attacked. The beast roared as the monster flew towards him. The beast seized him and smashed him onto the ground. It shook, leaving ripples in the stone. But the monster was up in a flash. Eyes blazing. There was rage etched in each face. Their lips curled. Teeth bared. They punched and kicked. Tearing, ripping, gouging at each other. Each one fighting an enemy larger than they could imagine. Around them there were screams and shouts. Nobody could stop them. They rode the wave of hate.'

Then, out of nowhere, Jeda and Chris noticed a silver glint.

The beast dropped his arms and stood motionless. He clutched his stomach as he fell to his knees. The monster, panting heavily, turned and leapt out of an open window, scrabbling to get away as fast as he could over the grey cobblestones.

The beast held his position for several moments, as people gathered around him. Then unable to keep himself upright any longer, he fell backwards, toppling onto the cold stone floor. Slowly, the fur fell from him, his body grew smaller and his facial features rearranged themselves, as he transformed back into his original form. A thin, red line traced its way down the side of his mouth as he struggled to breathe. He coughed, and little red droplets flew out of his mouth and spattered onto the ground.

Jeda and Chris watched in horror as the young man's friends tried to help him up. The scene moved so incredibly slowly they could see everything. His eyelids trembled as he blinked. His lips parted as he fought to speak. Around them was the blurred movement of people, as they tried desperately to seek help.

'As the young man lay on the cold ground, he looked up and above him. He saw a magnificent castle positioned on a great rock. It was lit up in all its glory. He saw the vague forms of his friends around him, as they tried to stop the flow of blood. He looked to the sky and heard the stars calling him. The wind was approaching and, anxious not to miss it, he mouthed his final message home.'

Jeda and Chris knelt by him. Silent tears flowed down Jeda's face. She stroked his hair, placing one hand on top of his own, and heard the word fall from his lips.

'Mama.'

The wind scooped up the message and carried it. He had completed the one thing he needed to do, then Jeda saw his arms fall by his sides. She watched his eyes close. She saw his chest still. His body slowly fragmented into a thousand tiny shards of light, which began to float gently, sparkling and twinkling, towards the moon.

'The wind blew tenderly. It knew the importance of this message and so delivered it with grace a few days later. In a faraway land, where the sand shimmers like gossamer, a woman was preparing a meal fit for royalty. A breeze caressed her face and she heard the word 'Mama'. It was evening and she smiled and gazed upwards, when suddenly she became aware of a bright new star sparkling and shining. It was so brilliant, it reflected the

planets, the universe, the infinite. It reminded her of how much she missed her son. How she longed to hold him. But she reassured herself that by the brevity of his message he must surely be thriving in the beautiful Land in the Sky.'

Jeda struggled to hold in her tears. She found her feet lifting off the ground and she started floating into the air. She tried to grab at something to steady herself, but saw that her father was experiencing the same sensation. As they moved upwards, both noticed their feet begin to disintegrate into tiny dust particles and then blow away into nothing.

Chris was filled with panic.

'My feet! My feet! Help!'

But it continued higher up his body. His knees soon disappeared, then his thighs, his chest, his shoulders and finally his head.

Jeda closed her eyes, accepted her fate, and disappeared.

WAR OF THE WORDS

When Jeda opened her eyes she found herself lying on the floor of the hallway outside her room. Her father was passed out cold right next to her. Her mind filled with images of the young man and what had taken place. She immediately stood up and went to wash her face to clear her mind. As she clutched the sink with both hands, she peered into the mirror, but the eyes that peered back were not her own. They glinted wickedly.

The lips of her reflection mouthed the words, 'Hello, Jeda.'

It felt like an eternity since she had seen the Shadowman. She thought she had succeeded in keeping him under control, yet here he was. As she gazed at her reflection, the Shadowman grew bolder. It was still not too late. She was listening.

As he studied her face, he wondered how he could regain control. The stories were powerful and had certainly awakened something in the girl. As he looked her up and down, she appeared different. She stood taller. She was more sure of herself. He cursed the box. Although he had been unable to influence her in someone else's story, he had tried to infiltrate in different ways. He was everywhere – nobody could escape him – but somehow he had failed. The knot inside him burned with this knowledge. But all was not lost. Not yet.

'Jeda, I have missed you,' he began.

But Jeda knew his game. 'Leave me alone,' she cried.

'I cannot. I am a part of you,' he gently insisted.

'I don't want you!'

'You need me. Who else will keep you safe? There are monsters out there, or don't you remember?'

Jeda thought back to the young man with the sparkling eyes and the one with the furrowed brow. They both had a Shadowman. She realised then that he could never disappear. He was destined to stay, either in her or in another.

'With me, you will never be alone,' he encouraged.

But she knew deep down that he was completely wrong. She was never alone. She came from a great family. She understood that the world was hers and only she could forge her path through it. She did not need him. Ever!

She knew what she had to do.

She placed her fingers inside her mouth and then pushed her hand to the back of her throat. She gagged, but continued till her hand was deep in her chest. Her fingers sought out the Shadowman and, although he wriggled and tried to escape her clutches, she grabbed hold of him and pulled him out, writhing. She flung him to the ground, a moist, seething, pulsing creature. He glared at her, unable to disguise his contempt and hatred. He trembled and shook, furious at having been cast aside.

Jeda lunged at him, but he skipped out of her way.

'You think you can get rid of me?'

She tried again, but the Shadowman lowered his head and smiled cunningly before transforming into a mirror image of Jeda. He began to circle her.

'I am a part of you, Jeda,' he smirked. Then, leaning forward, he enquired with a raised eyebrow, 'You don't honestly think you can destroy me, do you?'

In frustration, Jeda roared, then seizing a nearby potted plant she flung it in his direction. He jumped to the left, spewing out mocking laughter as he did so. She snatched up her father's beloved soapstone elephant and threw it with all her strength, but he magicked himself out of the way, appearing right behind her. She rushed at him, slicing through the air with a wooden walking stick, but he dodged each blow with such ease and delight it infuriated her even more. He then cackled and whooped as though enjoying some great game, as cushions, books, ornaments, wooden and glass picture frames flew through the air. Jeda was exhausted. As she bent over to catch her breath, she caught sight of the little box.

The thin gold band appeared worn and faded. The wood was scratched and there were little chips along the edges, yet it was the most beautiful and precious box in the world. She picked it up.

'It is of no use to you now,' the Shadowman pointed out, as he crossed one leg over the other, leaning casually against a wall.

Jeda thought of her mother. She imagined her sitting in her bed pouring the stories in. She understood her reasons. The greatest gift she could leave her was a knowledge of self and, as she considered what the stories had given her, she realised that she did possess a weapon. The weapon of words.

She looked up and stared directly at the Shadowman. He did not like this. It was too defiant. He stood straight and stared back at her, a snarl itching at his lips.

Jeda took her words and began to mould them deep inside her. When they were perfectly formed, she unleashed them straight at him.

'Why are you threatened by me?'

The weapon flew from her mouth, through the air and hit the Shadowman in the gut with a sickening crunch. Immediately the Shadowman began to hiss and spit. He bent over and Jeda circled him. In defensive mode, he moved around the room, emitting low warning growls.

'What do you gain by bringing me down?' she questioned. The words hit him with such force that he was knocked back, where he quivered and cowered against the wall.

'Stop it. Stop it!' he seethed. He appeared smaller in stature and, as Jeda stared at the pathetic creature in front of her, she recalled Aunty telling her, 'Don't forget the words of Wole: a tiger does not proclaim its tigritude, he merely pounces.'

She sensed the power of the tiger flowing through her veins and she strode toward the Shadowman, who shrank into a corner.

'You are afraid of me,' she stated.

'Get away from me,' he cried, his voice increasingly high-pitched.

'You are afraid of what you are without me.'

'No, it's not true. It's not true,' he pleaded, his voice breaking as he shrank several inches before her eyes.

'You have no power over me.'

The words flowed from her lips and, as each word pierced him, he became smaller and smaller in size until he was no larger than a cockroach. She picked him up between her fingers and placed him on the palm of her hand. He was livid, shouting, cursing and stamping his feet. He screamed the vilest of abuse but Jeda heard nothing, for he had lost his power.

'You are nothing to me,' she whispered, and with that she pursed her lips and blew him off her palm, where he turned to dust and floated away into nothing.

A smile hinted at the corner of her mouth and Jeda was filled with an intense feeling of calm. She decided to get some fresh air and, as she walked down the street, she looked around her with fresh, new eyes. Despite the grey cloud, she saw beauty, colour and possibility. Though her feet were rooted to the ground, she felt as light as air. She loved this feeling. She had rid herself of the Shadowman. She was free!

As she leapt playfully over the cracks in the pavement, she suddenly became aware of a faint presence around her. She stopped, keenly aware that deep under the ground, hiding in the cracks in the walls, concealed in the darkest of corners, the Shadowman still lurked. He had been badly wounded on this occasion. He knew that the girl was simply too powerful to attempt anything at this moment, so he tended to his wounds, dreaming of the day she would weaken and be his once more. Jeda raised her head and smiled knowingly. She knew he could return at any moment, and he would continue to exist in others as long as they let him, but she also knew that her stories were her power. And to defeat him would be simple – all she had to do was listen.

AUTHOR'S NOTE

This story has roots in *Blood and Gold*, a storytelling performance that I created for the Edinburgh Fringe Festival in 2019. My intention was to explore the legacy of colonialism and slavery from an alternative perspective.

Inspiration for these stories came from multiple sources – my own family history, world history, folklore, myths and legends from across the European and African continents, real life events that we have seen in news features around the world, some of which you may be familiar with and others less so. I hope the stories touch you, move you, make you wonder. Above all, I hope this book inspires you to understand the power of your own story. Open your box!